P/NCHED

INSPIRED BY A TRUE STORY

WRITTEN BY

WILSON C CARTER III

Green Ivy Publishing
1 Lincoln Centre
18W140 Butterfield Road
Suite 1500
Oakbrook Terrace IL 60181-4843
www.greenivybooks.com

Pinched/Wilson C Carter III
ISBN: 978-1-946043-81-8
Ebook: 978-1-946043-82-5

Inspired by a true story

DISCLAIMER

Some names, dates, locations, and identifying details have been altered to protect the lives of individuals.

***

"There is only one way to learn," The Alchemist answered. "It's through action. Everything you need to know you [will] learn through your journey."

-Paulo Coelho, *The Alchemist*

"Words are, in my not-so-humble opinion, our most inexhaustible source of magic. Capable of both inflicting injury and remedying it."

- Dumbledore, *Harry Potter and the Deathly Hallows* – J.K. Rowling

Contents

CHAPTER ONE

THE MUSTANG

The young man's name was Marco. He had just arrived home as dusk was settling in on the small town of San Pablo, Colombia. Illuminating the spring sky was a beautiful rosy sunset, slowly falling behind the distant mountains, causing the greenery surrounding his home to shimmer vibrantly with life. He could hear the crunching of the gravel as he walked up the driveway into his wood-and-tin shanty.

Famished from a long day at school and from working his fingers to the bone at the docks, he was happy to smell his mother's cooking. He quickly kicked off his old Nike sneakers at the front door and walked into the living room, tossing his backpack onto the couch. The second he heard the roaring engine pull up in the driveway, he mentally prepared himself for an inquisition from his father regarding the math test he had taken earlier that day. *I hate math*, Marco thought. *I just want to be rich. Who cares about calculus? It's not like I'm going to actually need it in life anyways. Besides, I barely have time to study anyway because of work.* Marco worked as a first mate on a local fishing boat to help his parents with the bills. At the age of twenty-one he was already a skilled sailor. His father had gotten him into the water, swimming, before he could even walk. He felt completely comfortable in the water as if it was where he was meant to be. Nothing could touch him while he was out there. It was his escape route for everything, his calming remedy.

"*A comer*, Marco!" his mother shouted from the kitchen, breaking his train of thought. Grinning, Marco quickly ran into the kitchen and sat down at the modest wooden dinner table, where everything was already set and the food was ready to be eaten. His beautiful mother's name was Gabriella. She had thick black curls and big brown eyes. She was known for her captivating smile and her heart of gold, which continuously showered the room with love. She brought over his favorite, *Pollo a la Manuela*, his grandmother's infamous recipe, fresh from the frying pot. She served Marco his plate of flash-fried chicken and mashed potatoes before lightly kissing him on the head. His father, a man so large he could bulldoze through a concrete wall, walked into the kitchen. He had light skin, blond hair, brown eyes, and a thick beard. Stumbling in with his briefcase he announced, "*Mi amor*, this smells great, I don't know what I would do without you." This made Marco and his mother smile. Marco always appreciated his parents' relationship and hoped that one day he would be so lucky. Marco's family did not have much, but they did have love.

Although, at the moment, as far as he was concerned, love was not very important. Money was the only thing on his mind while girls were a distraction. He wanted more and he knew he and his family sure did deserve more than what they had. Marco was blessed with his athletic build and was easy on the eyes with his dark handsome features and dashing smile. But more importantly he was fully confident, borderline cocky. With ambition in his eyes and kindness in his heart, he was the total package.

"How did your test go, Marco?" his dad asked.

Coming back to reality Marco stuttered, "Uh, it went OK."

"What do you mean by OK, Marco?"

"I mean it went OK. I'll find out after the weekend."

"Marco, OK is unacceptable. Only..."

"Success is acceptable," Marco interjected. "You've told me a million times." Marco's father was a very demanding man and had high expectations for his son. Marco knew it was out of love, but it put a lot of stress on him to be expected to win and excel at everything. But sometimes the only thing on Marco's mind was going off and finding new adventures.

"You know why I push you so hard, son. It is a tough and cruel world we live in right now and your education is something no one can ever take from you. Not even those damn Narcos." The statement surprised Marco. He rarely heard his father swear, and even more rarely did his father speak about Colombia's massive drug problem, especially at the dinner table.

It was the spring of 1997, and the political situation in Colombia was very dangerous. Paramilitary groups and cartels were becoming increasingly powerful and dangerous and very, very rich. Both funded their violent operations through the sale of the world's favorite and very profitable narcotic, cocaine. The pueblos were welcoming them because they brought food and protection, but with the good came the bad. Murderers and rapists could also be found among the ranks. It was a kill-or-be-killed world the Narcos lived in, and much of Colombia was terrified of them. Even

Marco's father had to pay a "tax" to keep them away, or they would come and do as they pleased.

"Why must you say that at the table!" Marco's mother glared at her husband.

"*Lo siento, mi vida,*" Marco's father replied. "Those thugs have been increasing their demands on us, and it is so frustrating. They run around and do what they want and no one does a damn thing, especially not the government!"

Having finished his dinner and having heard his father's complaints before, he softly asked, "May I be excused from the table? I want to go meet Gonzalo out by the soccer fields."

With her face on her lap, his mother replied, "*Si,* mi amor."

Grasping his opportunity to escape further academic questioning, Marco rushed to put his sneakers back on after gently brushing off a spider that had found its way onto his laces. He was used to spiders. They liked making their webs in the dark corners of his home. He started off on his quick journey to the park.

It was nightfall as Marco walked at a brisk pace on the dirt road that led to the park. He felt comfortable in his barrio. He knew everyone in his tight-knit community but it was wise to be vigilant, especially at night, in this neighborhood. There were a lot of people far worse off than he was who may be hungry enough to do anything. The clouds covered the sky as they sometimes did on spring nights, making this evening especially dark.

He spotted Gonzalo on the other end of the soccer field. Some flickering park lights and a nearby drug store faintly illuminated his pale face, green eyes, and curly red hair. Marco had met Gonzo in grade school. Gonzo was being beaten up by a couple of bullies in an empty classroom when Marco came to the rescue. He pushed one to the ground and kicked the other one's legs out from under him. Marco wasn't the biggest but he was brave and tough as nails. The bullies left in haste and Gonzo quickly befriended Marco after that, sticking to him like a loyal puppy.

Marco shouted, "Gonzo, pass me the ball." Gonzalo kicked the soccer ball into the air, toward Marco, with accuracy that Marco wasn't accustomed to seeing from his goofy friend. "You've been practicing, huh, Gonzo."

"It's God given, I don't need practice," Gonzo replied slyly.

"Yeah, you wish." Marco laughed. "So what do you want to do tonight?"

"Do you remember Juan Ortiega?"

"I haven't seen him since we played soccer as kids. Didn't his brother join the cartel?"

"Yeah, but Juan's cool. He told me he didn't get into that."

"Why would he tell you if he did?" Marco said sarcastically.

Gonzo raised his voice. "Because there's two kinds of people in this world, Marco, those who get fucked and those who do the fucking." He threw a jab and an awkward-looking kick at an imaginary enemy.

Marco laughed at his ridiculous friend. "What does that have to do with anything?"

"I don't know," Gonzo said, laughing, "but he said if I drop off some car in Cartagena for him, he'd give me two hundred thousand pesos. I'll give you fifty thousand if you come with me."

Marco pondered it for a moment. "I want half."

"Fine." Gonzo groaned.

"Awesome, let's do it!" Marco knew Gonzo could use the money to help his parents and maybe buy a little joint after the stressful week he had just conquered.

"OK, let's go," Gonzalo said.

The boys started walking toward the town center, taking turns juggling and passing the ball back and forth. Watching Gonzo run was entertainment in itself; it took everything Marco had not to laugh at his friend. "He lives right down here," Gonzo said, about fifteen minutes later, as they turned down an alley, moving into an even more dangerous part of town.

OK, good, I was starting to wonder, Marco thought. They arrived at a rundown gray brick home with barricades on the windows and an iron fence surrounding the exterior.

Gonzalo whistled and yelled, "JUAN!"

Dogs started barking as movement could be heard inside the home. The iron doors rattled open as a shirtless young man covered in tattoos walked toward the gate, unlocking it and allowing the boys to enter. He was wearing a ridiculously large gold chain around his neck and ripped jeans that hung low and would probably fall off if Juan weren't holding them up. "Hola, Gonzo, I am glad you came, homie, I was thinking about giving the opportunity to someone else," Juan said in a cocky tone as he lit a Marlboro cigarette. Marco couldn't help but feel a little uneasy. He had met Juan before but very briefly at a soccer game, and it had not been a friendly meeting. Juan was a bit older than Marco and played dirty. He was the kid that would slide into you, trying to hurt you, when going after the ball. He was the kind of guy Marco's parents always advised him to avoid.

Juan glanced up and down Marco, sizing him up. "You're taking this fag with you?" Juan asked Gonzalo with a surprisingly friendly grin, obviously kidding. The boys laughed and followed Juan to the poorly built garage.

Inside they found a blue 1969 Ford Mustang GT convertible with white racing stripes and a cream interior. Marco's mouth dropped open. It was more than rare to see such a nice car in this part of Colombia, outside of magazines. He couldn't help but appreciate its beauty.

"So, all you have to do is bring this to Cartagena and drop it off at this address, then take the bus back." Juan passed a piece of folded paper to Gonzalo. "Here's the keys. I'll let them know you're coming, and don't take too long or they'll be pissed."

"Who's *they*?" Marco asked.

Juan gave Marco an evil grin and closed his eyes to slits, giving himself a snakelike appearance. "*No te preocupese*, don't worry about it." He turned around and went inside, slamming the iron gate behind him, causing the dogs to bark again.

"What a douche," Gonzalo said. "He didn't even say bye."

"This might sound strange, but why does this guy have such a nice car?" Marco said.

"Oh come on," said Gonzo, "who cares why he has it, we get to drive it. Plus my family needs the money and so do you. Come on, Marco. I'll let you drive it first."

Marco looked at the car and couldn't help but want to drive it. The shine called to him and he wanted to feel the power of the engine. "OK, let's go. I don't want to get home too late."

The boys climbed in. Marco shut the door gently, afraid to mess up the beautiful car. Twisting the key, he felt the car come to life and roar. He could feel the engine's power already. This car was far superior to anything he had ever driven, and his body tingled with excitement. He threw the car in reverse and got them onto the road. Shifting gears into first then second he proceeded, en route to Cartagena.

Once on the open road he increased gears to see what the car could do. The engine thundered as the boys cruised down the highway. After about twenty minutes on the road, Gonzalo was eager to drive so they pulled over and switched spots. Gonzalo drove the rest of the way into the city.

Cartagena is a beautiful coastal city that is vibrant with color and festivities. There is always live music and plenty of cheap drinks to go around. Littered with beautiful women and scenic beaches, it's a bachelor's paradise.

Marco had spent many weekends in Cartagena growing up as it was so close to his home that the family, and even groups of friends, could make a quick weekend getaway when money was available.

Gonzalo looked at the address on the paper and conceded he was lost, allowing Marco to direct them to the building. They pulled up to a beautiful white gate that was surrounded on both sides by greenery. Gonzo pulled up to the gate and spoke to the guard. "Hola, we were told to bring this car to this address, but we could be wrong. I am not sure." The guard, who was wearing camo and had an assault rifle draped over his shoulder, looked at them curiously. Without saying a word he grabbed a piece of paper from inside his security box and went to the back of the car to check the license plate. He scribbled something down on the paper and went back into the guard box. They heard a buzz and the gate began to rattle open. The guard saluted them and Gonzo gave him an unsure "gracias."

They slowly drove the car along the gravel road, taking in the grandiosity of it all. The front yard had palm trees, flowers, and fountains, which were illuminated by garden lights, giving everything a majestic look. The beautiful white mansion's walls were hugged with vines and held up by pillars. Servants could be seen attending to their responsibilities. Iron bars surrounded the entire estate with armed guards patrolling. It was a seaside manor; Marco could smell the salt in the air. This home looked like a palace for a god.

"Where are we?" Marco whispered. He had never seen a house like this before. The guards seemed to recognize the car and waved them into the garage. An iron door slammed shut behind them, encasing them in the poorly lit garage. One of the guards told them to wait. The boys looked at each other. Neither could formulate a sentence. The guard turned the light on before leaving through a side door. The bulb illuminated the garage, showing a massive room that held all sorts of toys: a pair of red and black Suzuki motorcycles, a brand-new blue 1998 BMW, ATVs, fishing spears, fishing rods, and scuba tanks.

Marco's jaw fell as he began to look around. He had never seen so much wealth in his life. Realizing how stupid he must look with his mouth open, he shut it. "What the hell is going on, Gonzo?"

"I have no clue, brother," was all his friend could muster in reply. Gonzo tried to reposition himself in the car, ripping his sneaker on the side of the door. "Shit, these are brand new. I saved for months to buy these."

"What did it get caught on?" Marco asked.

"Umm, I don't know... this little piece of metal right here, piece of shit!" Gonzo kicked the side of the door, causing the metal panel to shift. "That's weird, you would think a Mustang would be properly welded."

Marco leaned in closer to examine the metal. It looked to him like it had been welded after it had been bought. He pushed the plate, causing it to fall off, revealing a secret compartment. This was no ordinary car. It had been tampered with. "Who would do that to a Mustang?" Marco asked.

Gonzo's face became paler than ever as the little bit of color he had quickly vanished. "Marco," Gonzo whimpered. "Look around, who in Colombia has this kind of money..."

Marco's breathing became short and rapid as, piece by piece, the puzzle seemed to come together. They weren't transporting a car at all but its hidden contents. They could be transporting drugs, or guns, or money, or maybe even a dead person in the trunk. *Shit, I didn't check the trunk. Who knows what could be in there?* Marco thought. "Gonzo!" he whispered. "We need to leave now. This is a Narco car. We need to leave before they come back."

"You're crazy," Gonzo replied with nervous laughter. "It's just a car. We're fine. Juan wouldn't do that to me."

"Juan doesn't give a shit about you!" Marco hissed at him.

Just then the garage door opened and a short and muscular man in a well-tailored white suit came through the doorway followed by two thuggish-looking guards carrying assault rifles. Marcos heart dropped into his stomach. "Please get out of the car, gentlemen," the man said kindly as he walked behind the car, two fingers gliding along the exterior of the trunk.

Marco and Gonzo got out of the car and stood in front of it, terrified.

"Cho Chi, give them their pay." Obediently, one of the guards handed Marco a wad of cash.

"Please," Marco pleaded as calmly as he could, "we didn't know what we were doing. The hatch fell by itself. We thought it was just a car. Please, I don't want the money, just let us go home and no one will ever know." Gonzalo stood next to Marco, quivering and hyperventilating, too afraid to move or speak.

"You will take the money, you earned it, kid. How old are you?"

"No, I won't take it, I don't want it." Marco was getting angry.

The man in the white suit's expression quickly changed from kindness to anger. He took out a revolver he had holstered underneath his jacket and pointed it at Marco's head. He spoke softly but firmly. "Listen closely, boy, I do not have time for your insolence, you will learn some respect. You will take the money. You will come back next week. Then again the week after, then the week after that if I damn well choose. If you do not, or if you tell anyone, we will find you and kill you and your family. Look me in the eye, boy," the Narco growled.

Marco looked up into his eyes and saw only darkness in the man's soul. His face was scarred and clean-shaven and reminded Marco of a bulldog. Gonzo continued to tremble next to him.

"I have the power to make you disappear or the power to make you a very rich man. That is your choice." The man shifted his gaze and directed his pistol to Gonzalo. "You are a coward, we have no place for cowards here." He squeezed the trigger one time. BANG! The pistol fired one bullet, hitting Gonzo between the eyes. His face spattered and his body collapsed.

"NO!" Marco screamed while jumping at the man. The guards quickly restrained Marco before he could even touch the man in the white suit.

The guards kicked the backs of his knees, causing Marco to fall to the ground. They backed off, raised their guns, and pointed them at Marco as Gonzo lay lifelessly on the floor. Blood had begun to paint the floor red and engulf the garage with its scent. "Please don't kill me," Marco pleaded. The man grabbed Marco by his shirt collar and pointed his gun at Marco's temple. He spoke to Marco with venom coating every syllable. "I am The Patron. I am the boss. My name is Carlos Castano and you belong to me now. *Ese aire que estas respirando, ahora es mi aire,* the air you breathe into your lungs, is now my air."

CHAPTER TWO

THE CABIN

Marco woke up with a jolt. His heart began to race and his memory struggled to put together recent events. As his mind cleared, the pieces of the puzzle seemed to come together. Gonzo was dead. His stomach began churning, making him feel ill. He couldn't believe it. He held his head in his hands, holding back tears. He looked around at what would be his new home. Well, "home" was hardly a word for it. This new building felt foreign and cold, like a concrete box. He missed his mother and father and was worried about them. He had not even been given a chance to say goodbye.

After The Patron had subjugated Marco, he had ordered his guards to take him to a new location. Someplace called "The Cabin." Unable to combat the heavily armed soldiers, he had conceded. They put a dark bag on his head and stuck him into the trunk of the car so he wouldn't know where they were going. He attempted to feel when the car was turning and visualize where he was but quickly lost track. It was a short but very bumpy car ride. In reality it lasted about half an hour, but for Marco it felt like a lifetime.

Upon arrival he was incarcerated in this cabin, which would be his new home, and told to await further instructions. He tried to force himself to be brave. His father had once told him, "Bravery is not the absence of fear but rather being afraid and doing the right thing anyway." But it was to no avail. He was alone, miserable, and terrified. Marco fell asleep on an old thin mattress that lay next to what must have been a thousand kilos of 100 percent pure Colombian cocaine. There was so much. It was unbelievable. Bags piled six feet high from one corner of the room to the other. There were no windows and only a couple of light bulbs that actually worked. Marco was awoken from his daydream by the sound of the locks on the front doors being rustled. He got to his feet to take a look, all the while praying for his safety.

A giant man, about six and a half feet tall and 240 pounds, walked in followed by three smaller, younger men all looking around the same age as Marco. The large man was smoking a cigar. He wore camo pants and a black undershirt with an assault rifle draped across his back. "*Buenos dias, bitch*," he said in a deep angry voice. "Welcome to the Niños. Call me Oso, you report to me now. Understood?"

"Si, Jefe." Marco looked directly into his eyes.

"Good boy," he said in a degrading tone. "We know who and where your parents are, Marco. If you betray us we will find you and kill you. And then we will kill them." Oso smiled.

How does he know my name? thought Marco.

"These are your partners, Nico, Daniel, and Pitufo. If you have any questions, ask them." Nico was the tallest of the group with curly hair, blue eyes, and a thin build. Daniel was the darkest and shortest of the group, with a handsome face, and Pitufo seemed to be right in between them with a medium build and a bit of scruff beginning to grow along his jawline. His facial features gave him a rodent-like appearance. All of them wore military camo.

The boys all looked at Marco, giving him a nod. "Leave your feelings in the past, boys, we don't have time for that shit here. Prepare your eyes, mind, body, and soul because you are going to experience things like you never have before. Welcome to hell. I have shit to do, stay here and take care of the merchandise, *maricas*." With a puff of his cigar Oso turned on the heels of his boots to leave. "Oh, I almost forgot, here, you'll need this." He grabbed a pistol out of his side pocket and tossed it to Marco, who was barely able to snatch it by the barrel before it fell to the ground. Oso let out a laugh and then disappeared through the front door, slamming it as he left. The pistol felt strange in Marco's hands. He had never held one and, after what had happened to Gonzo, he didn't really want to.

"Do you know how to use that?" asked Daniel.

"Obviously not, look how he's holding it." Nico laughed.

"Great... we have a scrub." Pitufo sighed.

Who are these guys? Marco re-gripped the pistol by the handle and began to inspect it. It was unloaded, kind of heavy, and cold. It was a 9mm Glock. He began pointing it around the room.

Nico yelled at him, "Hey, retard, watch where you point that and take your finger off the trigger, you idiot." Marco smiled for the first time in what seemed like decades. The pistol made him feel powerful, and he wanted to fire it.

"Can you guys show me how to use this?" Marco asked the boys.

"Yeah, just don't shot me with it." Daniel lifted up his shirt, exposing a pistol, and motioned for Marco to walk outside with him. The other boys followed. "Keep your finger on the barrel until you intend to shoot," Daniel said. "Make sure to squeeze the trigger with the middle of your finger so that the barrel shoots straight. Even a millimeter to the left or right and you could easily miss your target, and out here that means life and death." Daniel seemed like a nice guy despite being a criminal. "Go ahead and try it out. I have extra ammo."

Marco looked around the outside of his new "home" and was surprised to see so much green. A small dirt path went as far as the eye could see but, other than that, they were surrounded by jungle. Marco spotted a glass beer bottle about fifteen yards away, at the bottom of some brush, and gave it a go. The bullet landed to the right of the bottle, scattering dirt in all directions. The boys chuckled.

"Relax your hands, you're too tense," Daniel said, "and don't squeeze the trigger so hard. That's what makes the bullet curve."

Marco took a deep breath and relaxed. He raised his new gun and confidently squeezed the trigger. Bull's-eye. The sound of shattering glass penetrated the silence of the forest with a loud bang.

The boys nodded in approval. "Good job." Daniel smiled. "Now let's see how you do with a moving target. Daniel picked up a few roofing tiles left next to the poor excuse for a house. With both hands he hurled the tile into the air. Marco aimed and shot, destroying the tile. *Hell yeah! Maybe I'll just shoot all these guys and run away. No, I cannot, I am no murderer, that's not who I am.*

"So what are you doing here anyway?" Pitufo scowled.

The brief happiness Marco had felt after successfully shooting a gun for the first time quickly disappeared as he was reminded of Gonzalo's brutal assassination. "They're forcing me to be here." Marco looked down at the ground.

"Really!?" Nico said. "I wanted to join. It's the best way to make real money. It's a real business opportunity. Plus I have to take care of my brother."

"It's the only way to make real money here," Pitufo said.

"Yeah, I guess that's true, and for Colombia, the A.U.C. is the future," Daniel said authoritatively.

"This is the A.U.C.?" Marco asked. He had heard about the organization from his father. The A.U.C. was a right-wing paramilitary group that funded its activities through the cocaine trade and whose ultimate goal was to unite the people of Colombia against the leftist paramilitary group the FARC and the corrupt national government of Colombia.

"Si," Daniel said. "The United Self-Defense Forces of Colombia, we fight for the people of Colombia. VIVA COLOMBIA!"

"VIVA COLOMBIA!" Nico replied.

Pitufo just sniggered and rolled his eyes.

"Why are you here?" Marco asked Pitufo.

"The money, man, the power, the women, the lifestyle. The A.U.C. run this part of the country. We do what we want when we want. Not even the government can stop us. Just gotta keep your head down and listen to The Patron and you'll get yours."

"But what about school?" Marco asked.

"Dude, shut up," Pitufo said. "Why the hell would I waste my time at school studying to get some shit job, go home to my ugly wife, and be miserable."

"Well, if your wife is ugly that's your fault." Nico snickered.

"Fuck off, Nico, you shit stain. The point is when you're with the Narcos you're protected and you get paid, bottom line."

"In my neighborhood," Daniel said. "We don't have power and a lot of the time even the water gets rationed. We can barely afford food so college isn't even an option. It's really the only way I can make sure my family doesn't starve."

"So you all chose to be here?" Marco asked. The boys nodded. *So why are they making me be here if so many people want to be here?*

The boys all sat down outside the cabin except Pitufo, who walked inside. "What's the deal with Oso?" Marco asked his new companions.

"We don't really know," Nico said. "All we know is he used to be in the national army so he's a deadly son of a bitch and can be a dick if he doesn't like you. But he's not that bad if you get on his good side. We don't know why he joined the A.U.C. though. Probably the money." Nico shrugged.

"What about your parents?" Marco asked.

"My father died fighting the FARC. They're the socialists who keep planting bombs and raiding farmlands. My mom likes to drink so I don't know where she is. She disappeared a few months ago, but whatever." Nico sighed, chucking a nearby stone into the brush. "I have my little brother and that's all I need. We take care of each other. I do this so he doesn't have to."

Daniel chimed in, "You should be proud to be part of the A.U.C. We're doing revolutionary things. We're going to make Colombia great."

"Shut that fat, ugly mouth, Daniel!" Pitufo was coming out of the cabin, clenching something in his fist. "Don't believe that propaganda garbage. Just focus on yourself."

"Shut up, you rat," Daniel retorted.

Pitufo gave him a slimy grin and pulled a knife from his pants. All the boys eyed the eight-inch silver blade Pitufo had just withdrawn. "Relax, you pussies," Pitufo said, looking around at the other Niños.

He opened his hand, revealing a baggy full of cocaine. He put the blade in his mouth and held it between his teeth as he opened the plastic baggy with both hands. He held the bag in place with his left hand and grabbed the knife with his right, releasing it from his teeth before dipping the front edge into the white powder. He used the knife to scoop up a bump, leaned forward, and inhaled it in his right nostril. "WOOO! That's some good shit!" He laughed, leaning his head back and pushing up on his nose. Marco had never seen someone do cocaine before and was a bit intrigued.

Nico and Daniel both looked very stern. "You're not supposed to do that," Daniel said.

"Who gives a shit?" Pitufo said. "You want some?"

"Kinda." Nico relaxed a bit. "But better not, we don't know when Oso will be back."

"How about you, rookie?" Pitufo offered Marco the blade and the baggy.

"No, I'm good."

"Great, more for me then." Pitufo shrugged.

"You're going to get us all killed," Daniel said with disgust.

"We're all going to die anyway." Pitufo chuckled. He leaned back into the dirt and let out a deep breath. Marco had had enough; he walked back inside the cabin to calm his racing mind. He knew he was not prepared for the adventure he had just begun.

CHAPTER THREE

THE TRANSPORTER

Half asleep, Marco rolled to his side attempting to return to his dream. He was back home with his family watching the Colombian national soccer team play Argentina for the Copa America semifinals, and the teams were in overtime. He did not want to leave dreamland to face the reality of his new situation. It was hot and muggy and he had sweated throughout the night. He lifted his body off the old mattress and felt his skin peel away from the sticky cushion. He looked around and began to think.

A week had passed since he had been brought to the cabin, and Marco had been on his best behavior. He had tried to take in as much information from the other Niños as possible. It was necessary for his survival. His accuracy in shooting had continued to improve and, being an eternal optimist, he began to feel more comfortable with his new circumstances. By focusing on all the riches the other Niños spoke of, he was opening up to the idea that he would now be a member of the Auxiliary Forces but was committed to making sure he didn't lose himself along the way. It wasn't the ideal route to success, but a part of him loved the adrenaline that shot through his body whenever he heard a rustle in the woods or gravel being flung on the road. Usually it was just an animal doing as nature intended, but every couple of days Oso would come and check on the Niños, bringing news of victories the A.U.C. had won against the left-wing organization the FARC.

Slowly he and the other Niños were getting to know each other, but it was far from a love affair. Nico and Daniel seemed like great guys; they had hopes, dreams, and noble ambitions for after their time as Narcos but Pitufo, on the other hand, strictly fantasized about material things, power, and women. He had openly admitted to selling drugs when he was as young as eleven one night as he and Marco lay patiently waiting for orders. He had come from Medellin and had grown up when Escobar was still running the show. At fifteen he had killed his first man. It was a hit on some reporter. He had run up behind him in a restaurant, with his face covered by a T-shirt, shot the man in the back of the head, and sprinted for his life. Pitufo laughed while telling the story; it was disturbing to Marco. It was difficult for him to comprehend the lack of empathy a human could have for another.

Spring was quickly becoming summer, and Marco was beginning to get restless. He was completely sick of living in the forest. It was hot, sticky, muggy, and full of bugs. But he was too frightened to ask for a change.

Just then Marco heard the familiar movement of gravel at the end of the dirt road and glanced around the corner of the house to see what it was. Oso was pulling up in a massive black 4x4 truck. *This is new.* Trucks were unusual because they were so expensive and costly to maintain; it even had a cover over the bed. "*Buenos dias, putos!*" Oso shouted as he jumped out of the truck and started pulling back the truck bed cover. He seemed to be in a worse mood than usual. "Start loading the truck with the product." Dutifully the boys started hauling the twenty-five-kilo bags of blow onto the bed of the truck. They formed an assembly line to make the transfer more efficient.

"Sir, what's happening?" Marco asked.

The nervousness in his voice seemed to soften Oso. He smiled for the first time. "Nothing, Niño, this product is just ready for transport. El Patron ordered it and you guys are being relocated. The boss needs you guys to start working! You will be paid for your time here once we get back to Cartagena. Then each of you will be given a route to a city. Transporting will be your new job. The Patron will give you more details later."

Marco and the other boys nodded. As Marco loaded the truck with cocaine, his brain buzzed with ideas. Not sure if it was from being surrounded by cocaine or from the good news, he couldn't help but smile at the thought that he would be leaving the jungle, getting paid and, hopefully, getting to shower, and he was getting a promotion. *What a great day! Transporter? What will I be transporting?* The answer came to him as quickly as the question itself as he looked down at the snow-like substance he was carrying. *Oh. Shit. But I don't want to...* He gazed at the pistol strapped at Oso's side and realized he didn't have a choice. He knew he couldn't fight the Narcos, not even the government could. He couldn't run. They would find him and kill him and his family, and the thought of his loving mother and father suffering the same fate as Gonzo was too much to bear, so he stayed put.

Although, to be honest, a part of Marco enjoyed his new lifestyle. The adventure, the danger, the unknown, and the money were all appealing to him. He knew what he was doing was wrong, but who was really going to stop them? His paramilitary organization was so powerful and wealthy they essentially ran the country. *My paramilitary organization.* The idea felt foreign although, admittedly, he was beginning to feel a bit of pride regarding his new status and title, knowing he was untouchable wherever he went. He had visions of himself covered in money. The food, the clothes, the toys, and the women would all be available to him. It was cool to think about. He had visions of himself drinking beers on his own boat in the ocean and then docking it at his mansion home with his supermodel girlfriends awaiting him, just like The Patron.

Ripping him out of his delusions of grandeur was the memory of Gonzo having his head blown off. Shivers shot up his spine. That quickly brought him back to earth, and all his joy and excitement swiftly vanished. His focus became sharp. He knew he must remain vigilant at all times in order to survive. He had spent a lot of time pondering the best course of action during his time in the cabin and had come to the conclusion that the best way to thrive in this situation would be to gain favor with the A.U.C. and have them trust him. After all he had no choice; they owned him and it was not only his life he had to protect but his family's as well.

CHAPTER FOUR

THE MANSION

Marco and the other Niños arrived, late that afternoon, at a rustic house on the outskirts of Cartagena. It was a large plot of land overlooking a beach that looked similar to Playa San Pablo, a beach Marco used to visit occasionally with his family. The only difference was that this house had armed guards patrolling the exterior. Oso drove them into the compound and ordered the Niños to get out of the truck and walk into the garage. As the boys entered they were awestruck. Waiting inside were four brand-new Suzuki GSX-R1100 motorcycles.

Marco grinned; he had always wanted a motorcycle. "These are now yours, Niños, take care of them. You will use them whenever you are told. Now hop on and learn fast because you are going to ride them to El Patron's to await further instructions." Oso tossed each one of them a set of keys.

Enthusiastically, Marco hopped on his shiny new black bike. He turned the key and heard the engine rumble; it felt like a beast. The other boys quickly did the same. He gave the engine a little rev to hear the motor roar. *Wow,* he thought while striking back the kickstand, shifting the clutch into first gear, and gently engaging the throttle. He slowly began rolling forward.

"Here is the address," Oso shouted above the engines, handing a piece of paper to Marco. It read:

Cra51 #80-85

Cartagena, Bolivar

Colombia

Marco gave Oso a nod and off he went. Once on the road Marco allowed himself to become acclimated to the bike. He swayed left and right on the street while he rode ahead of the pack. He was a natural. *I'll give it some gas when I am on an empty street.* He checked the side mirrors and saw his companions doing the same. "Screw it." Marco pulled down on the throttle and felt the bike speeding up. *Wow this thing is fast*, he thought as he flew way ahead of the pack. The trees on either side of him began to blur, as did the road ahead of him. He was quickly losing sight of the other Niños and let go of the throttle. He slowed down to await the other Niños. He couldn't help but smile. When the other boys reached Marco, they continued as a unit the rest of the journey, taking turns giving their bikes a bit of gas and practicing basic maneuvers. Pitufo surprised everyone when he did a wheelie.

Shortly after they arrived at The Patron's mansion, Marco soon became anxious as he remembered his last experience at the estate. The armed guards waved them in. *I guess they're expecting us. I wonder if he will say anything to me about last time.* The boys glided to a halt in front of the garage, and one of the guards led them to the front door. "Nice wheelie, Pitufo, where did you learn that?" Marco asked.

Pitufo gave him a sly smile. "My cousin had a dirt bike growing up, they're basically the same." A pretty maid greeted them and asked them to please remove their shoes at the front and wait in the living room.

The mansion was gorgeous. A brilliant chandelier hung above them in the foyer, and dual spiral staircases led up to the second floor. It was the kind of house Marco had only seen in movies. They walked to the left into the living room where they sat to wait. Plush leather couches adorned with exquisite furs decorated the living room. Another impeccable chandelier lit it. A fireplace gave it a homey feel and above that hung an enormous television. The floors were made of wood and all the end tables and coffee tables had granite countertops. Massive windows and glass double doors led to the backyard. An enormous infinity pool and hot tub overlooked the ocean. It blew Marco's mind that such wealth could exist. For the most part all he had ever seen was poverty.

Four men walked down the winding stairs before Marco could absorb the enormity of the house. The Patron was accompanied by four men who looked like they were in their mid-thirties. One of them was a short, tan, clean-shaven man, who asked The Patron, "Who are they?"

"I'll introduce you when they earn it, Jorge, now is not the time, my friend." The Patron calmly led three of the four gentlemen outside, shook their hands, and gave each a hug in turn. It was a softer side Marco had not believed was possible in such a man. The same man who, only weeks ago, had not even flinched before killing his friend.

El Patron and a second man, wearing a blue button-up shirt, slacks, and a gold watch, came into the living room with the Niños. The boys all stood up so Marco followed suit.

"OK, gentlemen, let's get to business," El Patron said sharply. "You will each be charged with a city. You will pick up packages and drop off packages. These packages contain my money, not your money. Do not mess with my money. You will be paid separately. Each of you will pick up the money in your respective city and bring it to my associate Ricardo here."

"Hello boys," Ricardo said very enthusiastically.

El Patron continued, "You will hide the package as best you can. If you are stopped, you will do whatever you can to make sure nothing happens to my money. Kill or be killed, that's Narco law. Although I presume none of you will be stopped because you will be driving too fast to be caught. I hope you enjoy your new toys; they are an investment in you that we believe will pay off. This money is your life. If a single motherfucking dollar is missing, you will be too. You will be given apartments in your respective cities to live in and to store the money when needed."

He pulled a piece of paper from his pocket. "Marco, you will be picking up from Santa Marta and bringing to Cartagena. Daniel, you will be delivering from Barranquilla to Cartagena. Pitufo, from Medellin to Cartagena and, Nico, you will be bringing it from Valle du Par to Cartagena. If someone tries to rob you, there better be a few bodies to be found or you better be dead or near dead, or else we will assume you tried to rob us. *La plata o tu vida*, the money or your life, Niños.

"You will be carrying, on average, five hundred thousand American dollars. Oso will give each of you your addresses, and I presume he has already given you your guns." The boys nodded. "Great, you will be paid in dollars."

Marco's eyes widened; dollars were basically gold in Colombia. The other boys had a similar response. El Patron clasped his hands together and smiled at their reaction. "You will be paid very well, Niños. Look around, this can all be yours one day if you are loyal and work hard. We have a lot of confidence in you, and we hope you will take this very seriously. No drinking, no drugs, and beware of women. Each of you will be given four bodyguards to protect you in your cities, they should be awaiting your arrival."

As Marco struggled to process all the new information and responsibilities, he noticed a girl, in the background, walking up from the ocean. A gorgeous girl in a white bikini, with long black hair, that made his heart beat even faster than it already was. He snapped out of it before El Patron noticed.

"And don't mess up or it will be your life. Any questions?"

"No, senor," said the Niños in unison.

"Good. Ricardo will give you your new home addresses in your cities. You may collect your pay in the kitchen. There will be envelopes on the table. You may see yourselves out. Let us know if you need anything. VIVA COLOMBIA!"

"VIVA COLOMBIA!" all the boys shouted in unison.

CHAPTER FIVE

HOOD RICH

Marco happily received his new address from Ricardo and his earnings from the kitchen and exited the mansion. Inside the package was a wad of cash and piece of paper, which he unfolded, revealing an address.

Cra 60 #72-80

Santa Marta, Magdalena

Colombia

He said goodbye to the other boys and, with his new wealth in hand, jumped onto his bike. He drove away from the mansion and toward Santa Marta as quickly as he could. He had been there once on vacation, to visit Tayrona Park, so he knew the route: just follow the highway along the coast. It was a beautiful seaside drive. He was still processing all the information he had just received from The Patron. He was astonished by the turn his life had just taken. He had gone from a broke fisherman to a Narco with a respectable amount of money in less than a month. *But at what cost? Who am I becoming?*

He geared up to increase speed, excited to get to his new home. He quickly passed Barranquilla and jealously thought about how Daniel had a much shorter route than his and how Pitufo had gotten Medellin, which was rumored to be full of gorgeous women. He didn't know, though, he had never actually left the coast of Colombia. He tried to focus on the positive. Santa Marta was known for its beautiful beaches, and he was soon smiling at the thought of himself sitting by the ocean catching some sun, drinking a beer, and piling stacks of cash.

The sun glared in his eyes and he made a mental note to stop and buy some sunglasses; he could finally afford them. He realized he was starving and resolved to treat himself to a delicious steak dinner that night, or every night, with what he had just made. *I might be able to ask for time off and travel now.* Money made everything that, at one point, had been so far out of reach completely possible. Marco daydreamed about all the new toys he could buy, the trips he could take, and the faraway places he could now afford to visit. He could go to Paris and see the Eiffel Tower or go to Rome and see the Coliseum. Maybe even take his family on a trip around the world. He smiled at the thought of being on an airplane for the first time and feeling the aircraft take flight. The idea of flying consumed his mind the whole trip until he realized he had to get off at the next exit to arrive at his new apartment complex.

Marco pulled into the plaza and found the building the directions had led him to. It was a tan and burgundy four-story beachside residential building. Marco was more than satisfied with the idea of having a beachfront apartment. As Marco drove into the parking lot, four gruesome-looking men in undershirts, cut T-shirts, and jeans were leaning on a brand-new-looking black Jeep, staring him down. All of them had tattoos and were drinking beer and smoking cigarettes. They had dark skin and Marco knew they were thugs. He could see their guns poking out of the Jeep. Not the kind of people he wanted to mess with.

"Ayo, Niño," shouted one of the guys. "You Marco?"

"Si."

"OK, *Jefe*," The largest one said.

"Jefe? Who are you?" Marco asked timidly.

"We're your bodyguards, we'll be looking out for you."

"Yeah, we got you, Jefe, anyone runs up in here we'll pump them full of lead. You let us know if you need anything, *a la orden*," the one with gold teeth said. *A la orden? At your service? I can get used to that.* The cautiousness he had felt about the men immediately lifted. He felt safer knowing he had bodyguards. These were his *sicarios. Awesome.* Just weeks ago he had been worried about a math test, and now he had respected sicarios at his service.

Pride swelled in his chest as he realized these grown men were legitimately at his command. But he knew with that with respect came danger. Getting caught with half a million dollars of Narco money was a lot worse than bombing a math test. "Thanks, man," Marco said with half a smile, which only one of them returned. "Let me know if you want water or beer or something.

"Si, si, *mas cervesa!*" they hollered, laughing. One of them put some salsa music on and they began to dance. *They aren't as scary as they look.* One of them, a lean but muscular Colombian, flung something at him. Marco caught it with one hand; it was a key. "2B," was all the man said.

Marco nodded and walked up the stairs, excited to have a proper shower. He was long overdue and was starting to smell. He looked down at his clothes and realized he really needed to buy new ones. He was beginning to look homeless. His time in the cabin had taken its toll on them. Marco arrived at the second floor and found his door. He turned the key and entered. He was greeted with a furnished two-bedroom apartment. He flicked the light on and was delighted to find he had electricity. It wasn't always a sure thing in Colombia. He inspected his new home and was impressed.

It had a modern kitchen with every appliance necessary: a coffee maker, a toaster, and a microwave. The living room had multiple couches, a table, and an enormous TV. He even had a balcony, and he could leave the door open to allow the breeze to enter. Air conditioning was rare in Colombia, so he was used to the heat, but a nice seaside breeze was a game changer.

Everything was already decorated for him. His room had a made bed, with red silk sheets and a black comforter, a desk, a dresser, and a walk-in closet. The bathroom was all marble, and he even had a bathtub. He was living large. He tested the water and was happy to find he had the option of hot or cold water too. *Wow. That's awesome.* He had never had hot water in his house before. *I made it. I'm the man. If only my family and friends could see me now.* He started to sing and dance as he tested the water temperature, happily switching it back and forth between hot and cold. *But they can't,* a voice in his head hissed at him, *they probably think you're kidnapped or dead.* The materialistic happiness that had been flowing through him for the last few hours quickly evaporated and, although he knew he was protected, he felt alone. Marco stopped dancing and looked at himself in the mirror. He was covered in dirt and his eyes had bags from several nights of bad sleep. He could hardly recognize himself. His hair was tangled, his facial hair was unkempt, and even his eyes looked different. He looked older, harder. He gazed at his hands; they felt rougher, dirty, and callused. *Who am I becoming? Who do I want to be?*

CHAPTER SIX

THE FINCA

Marco awoke the next morning thirsty and sticky. It was hot and he had sweated in his sleep and needed water. Marco got up and walked into the kitchen. He grabbed a cup from the cupboard and poured himself a glass of water. He quickly finished it and poured another to sip on while he sat on his balcony to enjoy his new view. He decided to buy an air conditioning unit next time he got paid. Summer was here and the breezes came sparingly. *If I'm going to be a Narco, I'm going to be a comfy Narco,* he thought while admiring his oceanfront view. Luckily, he had a fan to keep him somewhat cool in the meantime.

He quickly became bored and hungry. He decided to explore his new city and get some food. He grabbed his wallet and keys to walk over to a nearby restaurant to grab a chicken empanada for breakfast before heading to his beach.

The surface sand was hot from the sun so he dug his feet in, to reach the cooler sand below, while examining his surroundings. The waves were rolling in hard so he knew to be careful not to be swept out by the current. He would stay close to shore today. The ocean had always fascinated Marco. Embarrassingly enough, he had actually been scared of it as a kid. He had been swimming with his father when something had nibbled his foot. He had jumped clean out of the water and hung onto his dad for dear life. In hindsight it was probably a harmless fish. The memory made Marco laugh.

He took off his shirt and removed his valuables from his pockets before making his way to the water. He dove headfirst under the first wave he saw. The ocean had a way of cleansing his body and soul. It was as if the salt in the water washed away all his worries. He tried to float on the water, but a wave immediately crashed on him, shooting water up his nose. He decided to catch some sun instead.

He returned to shore, refreshed. He wanted to check up on his things too. It wasn't a good idea to leave valuables by themselves on the beach. Someone was bound to come snooping around eventually, and it was common to have things stolen. Usually it was harmless kids who were very poor and looking for something to eat, but you never knew. Colombia could be very dangerous as Marco was learning more and more each day.

He spent an hour relaxing on the sand before realizing he didn't even know what day it was. The sun was beginning to fatigue him so, after cooling down one more time in the water, he grabbed his things and made his way back up the beach to return to his apartment.

When he returned home he saw Oso's truck. Marco spotted him nearby, chatting with his guards. Oso turned around and saw Marco "Aha! There you are. Go get changed. We have work to do!" Oso seemed to be in a good mood, which surprised Marco. Oso had never been truly mean, but he had never really been nice either. Marco rushed upstairs, took a brisk shower to rinse off the salt, grabbed some money, and changed his clothes.

He returned downstairs, waved goodbye to his guards, and climbed into Oso's truck. "Where are we going?" he asked.

"To the Finca, Niño"

"Huh?" was all Marco mustered.

"You will see." Oso directed his gaze toward the road. They spent the next ten minutes in silence. *This is the Oso I am used to.* Marco used the opportunity to learn the streets and landmarks he may need to know in the future. Santa Marta was a small town with a beautiful cathedral in the center. It came alive at night and on the weekends as families went to the markets to buy essentials, but one had to be careful on the outskirts as poverty was quite common. *And when there's poverty there's danger.* The two men were now driving past the outskirts of the town and could see the makeshift shanties made of plastic and sheet metal. Marco took a moment to appreciate all that he now had, which would not have been possible if not for the A.U.C.

Oso turned and drove down a dirt road that would have devoured any normal car. Marco finally understood why Oso had a truck. He looked behind him, into the covered bed, and saw boxes. *I know what that is.* Marco knew he had better get used to it.

Ten minutes down the dirt road, they encountered a gate with a dozen men armed with machine guns and a couple of young boys carrying pistols. The boys were not wearing any shoes. Most of the men were dressed in military camos, while others only sported the pants, but all of them had guns, including the children. As they drove closer Marco noticed they weren't wearing Colombian military camos as he had seen the national military wear in the past. These were different. These were the A.U.C. camos. They had an orange patch with bold black letters that read "A.U.C." on the arm.

"This is the gate to the Finca, Marco," Oso said. "All these men are our soldiers, even the young ones. There are a lot more on the perimeter, that we can't see, as well. We are in a secure area here." Oso pulled up to the gate, gave a wave, and was allowed through. All the men watched the truck carefully and pushed the gate closed immediately after they had passed.

To his right Marco saw a naked man bound to a tree with rope. The binding was wrapped tightly around his throat and ankles to hold him firmly up and against the tree. His arms were tied together behind him. Blood dripped down his whole body, and his breathing came in short shallow breaths. A knife was lodged between his ribs. His head slumped forward, his messy hair covering his face, and multiple wounds spread across his torso and legs. A man walked by and, without hesitation, removed the knife and stabbed him again in the stomach. The man lifted his head and let out a loud shriek. Fresh blood began running down the dying man's body as his head slumped back down.

Marco's eyes widened and he felt like he was going to be sick. "Welcome to the Finca," Oso said. "That man tried to steal two million dollars from us. Don't be like that man, Marco."

Marco couldn't take his eyes off the man and continued watching, in the side-view mirror, as his head swayed, spitting up fresh blood.

Oso continued down the dirt road. There were armed men on either side every few hundred feet, and little houses and barracks littered the side of the road. The Colombian mountains seemed to be growing and they saw more structures as they went farther. "Mother Colombia protects us with her mountains too, the only way in and out of this Finca is down this road," Oso said.

Marco saw mostly men although there were some women and children working as well. The men were hard at work hacking plants and mixing, drying, and cooking chemicals. The women were bagging and organizing the cocaine. The children were in massive steel tubs stepping on the coca leaves. There were cocaine stations everywhere. It was a massive and admittedly impressive operation.

Marco could hear the ocean and he soon smelled the salt in the air. Oso parked the truck near the beach and said, "Now we walk." They made their way to the ocean, where several speedboats were docked, swaying in the calm waters. They were beautiful vessels, thin built for speed. Each one was at least forty-two feet long and had five 250-horsepower engines. They were easily the fastest boats Marco had ever seen. "Those boats are incredible," he said.

"Have you ever been on a boat?" Oso asked with a deep chuckle.

"Yeah, I know how to sail pretty well, I used to be a first mate. I have been on the water pretty much my whole life," he replied with pride.

"Interesting," Oso said, scratching his chin, "good to know."

The location was beautiful. Blue water with fine white sand and encased by stunning mountains. It looked like a postcard. What could easily have been a tourist resort had instead become a massive cocaine operation. Now Marco understood why there were so many armed guards. Marco had to control his breathing to remain calm. He had never imagined it possible that he would be in this situation, but here he was.

"Wait here," Oso ordered as he walked onto the boat. Five minutes later he returned with a case and handed it to Marco. "You will bring this to Cartagena. Today your responsibilities also include helping me unload the truck and helping prepare this boat for launch. I need you here three times a week, Mondays, Wednesdays, and Fridays. I will pick you up myself. The rest of the time is yours to do as you please. The address to the delivery house in Cartagena is inside. Make sure every dollar arrives safely. Now throw that in the truck and help me with the cargo."

A few other men got off the boat as well and, as a unit, they hauled over four hundred bags of cocaine onto the boat. Each bag was twenty-five kilos so, between the five of them, they made quick work of it. The truck looked noticeably lighter as the bed rose, free of its cargo. "How much does each boat take and where is all this going?" Marco asked.

"Two thousand kilos and Honduras, Niño," Oso replied. "Pray you never have to escort it. That's when things get really dangerous. Wait here, I'll be right back and then I'll take you back home."

Marco nodded and began to pray, right then and there, that God kept him safe no matter what happened; he knew he was going to need it.

Marco looked around for something to distract himself with while he waited for Oso. He saw a group of kids passing a soccer ball around and jogged over to them. "Can I play?" he asked the children.

"Yeah!" squeaked one of the smaller ones, passing him the ball. Marco moved the ball around as each kid tried to take it back. He was easily twice their size and kept the ball with ease. None of them was wearing shoes, and only one had a shirt, a torn-up old 1972 Miami Dolphins Undefeated T-shirt. All the children giggled as the game of keep away continued until he overstepped, falling butt first onto the ground. Every child erupted into laughter, and Marco couldn't help but laugh at himself. Oso was walking his way and waving him over to leave, so he said his farewells to the kids and made his way to the truck.

Halfway home Marco finally mustered the courage to ask Oso about himself. After initial hesitation the mountain of a man relented a bit and explained to Marco how he had ended up in the United Self-Defense Forces of Colombia. He had started as a private in the Colombian Army when he was just eighteen. He was proud to say that he quickly rose through the ranks, in his twenties, to become a sergeant and was slated for future promotions. At this point in the story he became quite somber. He finished by saying, "I couldn't stand the corruption anymore. So I left and now I get paid a hell of a lot more for much less work." Marco could sense Oso was done speaking and decided it would be best to keep his mouth shut.

CHAPTER SEVEN

CATALINA

Marco woke up with a start in the middle of the night. He was sweating from a nightmare. He had been back in the garage with Gonzo and The Patron. Instead of enlisting Marco, The Patron had decided to kill him too. He had awoken just as Castano had pulled the trigger.

He lay in bed praying that everything he had experienced the day before had been a dream. He hoped, with everything he had, that when he opened his eyes he would be back in his home with his family. But he wasn't. He opened his eyes and looked around. Next to his bed he saw the briefcase full of money. He had counted it. It was $500,000. *How the hell am I supposed to take that to Cartagena three times a week? How are they making so much money? What the hell is going on?* He looked at the clock. 4:20 a.m. He had several hours before he had to make the trip. Oso had said to wait until dusk. It was safer at night. Fewer people on the road meant fewer cops on the road. "I'm screwed," he said out loud. Marco stared at the ceiling until he fell asleep again.

The heat woke him up around midday. He went down to the beach to cool off and grab some lunch. Deciding he was sick of waking up in sweat, he went and bought an air conditioning unit. He paid extra and in cash to have it installed that day. *If I am going to take all this risk, I am sure as hell going not going to wait to enjoy the benefits.*

As evening crawled ever closer, Marco heard a knock on the door. He opened it and was surprised to see a gorgeous girl waiting outside holding a bag. She had sun-kissed skin with long dark hair and emerald green eyes. She was shorter than him and perfectly curvy where it mattered. She was wearing a skin-tight red dress to show off her assets. It was working. She smiled at him and said, "hola." *Wow, she has a nice smile.* She walked right in and examined the apartment as if it were her own, ultimately taking a seat on his countertop and crossing her legs. She rested her chin on her fist and looked at Marco impatiently.

"Are you an angel?" he asked smoothly.

"*Prisa, chico*, let's go," she responded, having none of it.

"What? Where are we going?" Marco asked.

"I'm riding with you to Cartagena, Oso sent me. This is how it works. It looks less suspicious if there is a girl on the bike with you, duh."

"Oh, OK." He was taken by surprise but relieved he wouldn't be going alone.

He went into his room and grabbed the briefcase. He opened it to pull out the address. It read:

Cra 50 #62

Cartagena, Bolivar

Colombia

Maybe I should introduce myself. Yeah, that would be a good idea, idiot. He went back into the kitchen to greet her. He kissed her on the cheek, as was Colombian custom, and introduced himself. She stared at him, gave him a soft, seductive smile, and pulled a lollipop out of her bag. "My name is Catalina, put your case in my bag. I brought dirty clothes to cover it up and if anything happens we just say we're traveling. I don't think a cop is going to want to go through my thongs. That would be un-gentleman like. And I can be quite persuasive if I need to be." She licked her lips and gave the lollipop a little kiss before sucking on it.

Marco swallowed. *I'm in love.* "Good, we may need some persuasion," Marco replied, giving her his best seductive look and failing.

"Let's go, boy." She hopped off the countertop, grabbed the briefcase, and stowed it in her bag before heading for the door. Marco rushed to grab his motorcycle keys and followed her down the steps. "Those guys over there are dogs," Catalina said. They started whistling and shouting the second I got here." She looked at him softly. "You don't seem like that though."

Marco laughed and said, "No, my mother raised me better than that," while hopping on his bike. She put the bag between them and got behind Marco, grabbing onto him. He liked it. He liked this. This was fun. It was dangerous. How many other guys had beautiful women knocking on their doors and briefcases full of cash. *I'm the man.*

He floored the throttle and headed to the highway toward Cartagena. It was around 9:00 p.m. Oso had been right; the normally busy highways were almost dead. People didn't go out at night very often for they knew how dangerous it could be. There were thieves, Narcos, guerillas, thugs, and even crooked cops that would pull you over, make something up, and throw you in jail, if you didn't bribe them.

That thought was quickly dashed from his mind as he felt Catalina's right hand lower from his chest to his crotch. It shocked him a little and he gave a slight jolt. She giggled at him and then returned her hand to its original position. *I love my job.* Marco smiled. *I just have to make sure this money gets to Cartagena so I can keep it, and my life.*

Keeping up a great pace, Marco made it to the drop-off house in no time. The guards opened the gates for him without hassle and quickly motioned him into the compound. It was a large, impressive house but nowhere near as grandiose as The Patron's. The guard ushered him into the garage and closed it behind him. One guard asked for the briefcase, and Catalina handed it to him. Marco heard a doorknob rattle and saw Ricardo emerge from inside the house. He was as tall and thin as Marco remembered. He wore a red polo shirt and slacks and was beaming at Marco. "Marco! Thank you for bringing me the money!" He saw Catalina and said, "Hola, amor, don't you look just lovely tonight." The guard handed Ricardo the briefcase. "Normally, I don't come out for a small transfer, but I wanted to see how you were doing, Marco. Do you need anything?"

Why is he being so nice? Marco did his best to camouflage his thoughts. "No, senor, gracias."

"Well, you know what? Here's a little bonus. Take your girl here out for some fun on me."

Ricardo took out an envelope of cash and handed it to Marco. Marco took it, feeling cheap. He was realizing he was selling his life away. Every time he accepted money from these men, he was selling his freedom. But what could he do now? He had just transported half a million dollars for them. "Gracias, senor," was all he could muster.

"Fantastic, see you next time. Your real payment will be given to you back in Santa Marta. Great job, Niño, keep it up." Ricardo walked back into the house almost skipping. *That was weird.*

The guards told Marco he could leave, and Catalina hopped on his motorcycle and slid right behind Marco, pressing her breasts into his back. That distracted him a bit, not that he minded. They drove over to Cartagena's upper-class historic district to grab some dinner before heading back to Santa Marta. They decided on an elevated restaurant that had a beautiful scenic view of Cartagena, overlooked the ocean, and offered live music named *Café del Mar,* which just happened to be Catalina's favorite.

Catalina told him she had grown up in Cartagena but had moved to Santa Marta to go to school and to work a little. She explained her many aspirations, including the main one: being a nurse. "I want to study pediatrics; I just love being able to put a smile on a child's face." Her eyes grew wide. She chatted on about her goal of wanting to help people as much as she possibly could. "It's like a mother instinct in me, I just want to help." She had a burning desire to share parts of herself that she knew could make others feel better, and Marco liked that. He liked her more and more with every passing second. It was more than her beauty; there was something special about her. She made him want to be better and do more for the world. He decided to enroll in school too. He was making more money than he knew what to do with anyway, and he had the free time. A couple of classes wouldn't hurt.

He told her about his childhood and of his hopes and dreams of growing older. They talked of his family and of their vacations. He was cautious when explaining how he had ended up smuggling money for the A.U.C. and did his best to evade the subject entirely. He told her all of the places he wanted to visit when he could and was pleased she wanted the same. She wanted to travel the world too. They spoke for hours about all the adventures they could have before realizing the time and heading home.

They made the trip back seamlessly and arrived back at his apartment very late in the morning. "You can stay here if you want, or do you want a ride home?" Marco said.

She smiled and said, "OK," bouncing up the stairs. She walked right into the apartment, and Marco realized he had left it unlocked. *I really need to remember to lock this place.*

He went into his room and lay on his bed, exhausted, thinking about the day's events. He was proud he had successfully and safely completed his first transport. Marco heard a noise and saw Catalina slowly opening the bathroom door. She winked at him and posed seductively against the frame, wearing nothing but her red lingerie and heels, before cat walking toward him and fiercely staring into his eyes.

"I love my job," he said out loud.

CHAPTER EIGHT

THE PROMOTION

Summer left, and fall quickly followed. But that didn't change anything; in Colombia there are only two seasons: hot and hotter. Transporting became more than a routine to Marco. It was his life. He was gaining favor with El Patron and was making more money than he knew what to do with. Fall meant Christmas, and Christmas meant cookies, presents, and lots of family gatherings that Marco knew he would be missing out on. But he didn't feel too lonely because Catalina was right by his side, raising him up every time he felt low.

After months of hard work, Marco finished his first semester studying entry-level medicine. He hoped that maybe one day he would be allowed out of the A.U.C. freely and not in a box. He had become used to his new life but still felt the invisible chains the Narcos had on him. Sometimes the pressure was too much, and he had to go for long walks on the beach to clear his mind.

He always carried his pistol because he never knew when he might need it. He knew it was important to be optimistic, but it was more important he be aware of the very real danger he could be in at any moment and to be prepared. He knew fear was in his mind but acknowledged the peril he faced daily. It helped to know he had his bodyguards nearby in case anything happened. They usually worked in teams of at least two, although sometimes Marco was unsure how sober they actually were. They smoked a lot of cigarettes but sometimes he smelled a puff of marijuana, and he had gratefully accepted a joint from time to time.

The transports almost always went smoothly, but there had been a couple of trips where he had been forced to exponentially increase his speed when being tailed by mysterious cars or police. These days, his adrenaline was racing when he arrived home, and sleep would have been impossible had it not been for a little weed to calm his nerves. Luckily, no shots had needed to be fired, yet.

Originally, he had planned to use his extra bedroom as a man cave, but he was beginning to accumulate a lot of cash. There were cases of money, stacked on top of each other, throughout the room. Some were filled with pesos and others with dollars waiting to be laundered into pesos.

Catalina was also going to school, using the money she was making transporting with Marco. She was following her dream of being a nurse. She wanted to help others, which Marco loved, mainly because she had to take many of the same classes as he did, so she kept him up to date with assignments.

Marco still made the trip to the Finca to pick up the cash and help load the boats whenever Oso required, but the shock he had felt when driving in so many months ago had come and gone. It was a new normal for him to see thousands of kilos of cocaine in production, millions of dollars, and the occasional dead or dying body.

During his walks he would often revisit crucial memories, and those were the only times he fully comprehended the immense change in direction his life had taken in the past year. He also wondered what would happen next. Quite often, though, moving gravel or a shaking branch would snap him back to reality, and he would instinctively grab his already-loaded pistol. So far it was never more than a critter scurrying along in the bushes.

One day in early spring Marco was coming back from one of his walks. Today he had chosen to walk on the sandy beaches of Santa Marta to see and listen to the waves crash onto the shore. One had to be careful in Santa Marta's waters because the incredibly strong current and large waves had claimed many lives. It was a great for surfers, but for Marco the ocean helped him feel at peace.

When arriving at his apartment, he saw Oso waiting for him by his truck, arms crossed and not looking happy.

"What's up?" he asked.

Solemnly Oso said, "You have been promoted, grab your essentials. You won't be back for a while." Marco felt like he had been punched in the gut. Promotions in the real world were a good thing, but he had no idea what that meant in the sick world of drug trafficking.

"What if I decline and choose to just keep doing what I'm doing? I just got used to all this, I'm happy here."

"It's not an optional promotion, Niño. El Jefe needs you. Let's go, get in the truck. Everything is already prepared for you," Oso said sternly.

"This is bullshit," Marco said under his breath. *What am I going to do about school and Catalina? I won't even be able to say bye to her. She's going to think something awful happened.* This frustrated Marco the most. She had been such a great source of comfort to him; it really hurt him to leave her without saying goodbye. He couldn't even leave a note to let her know what had happened. He loved her and he had never gotten the chance to tell her. But he got in the truck. Oso could be incredibly intimidating. "Adios, mi amor," he whispered as Oso drove out of the parking lot.

In the past perhaps he would have let his emotions overtake him and shed a tear, but not anymore. His recent experiences had hardened Marco. He was no longer the boy he had once been. He was now a Narco, accustomed to pain and bloodshed. But although he would not show it, it gave Marco a heavy heart to leave the love of a good woman.

CHAPTER NINE

THE VOYAGE

Both angry and anxious, Marco stared out the truck window. Angry he was being forced to leave the small apartment he had come to know as home and anxious because he had no idea what to expect next. *The A.U.C. can give you everything and take it away in a second.*

"Where are we going?" Marco asked defiantly.

"The Finca, you will be transporting cargo, and watch your tone, Niño," Oso replied sternly. He let out a sigh. "Listen, Marco, it is not our place to question The Patron. Loyalty is the most important trait in this cartel. You will be rewarded handsomely for your services and punished dreadfully for insubordination. Make sure you do as you're told. You have seen how things go here, I don't need to tell you and, besides, I would hate for that to happen to you. You have a very bright future here. The boss always asks me how you are doing. So just trust the process and do your damn job. OK?" In the many months Marco had worked with Oso, those had been the kindest words Oso had ever said to him.

Marco forgot, on occasion, that many of these men weren't monsters. Just men who were pinched between a rock and a hard place. They needed money or had gotten caught up in making bad decisions. Like he had done. It was still mind blowing to Marco how one decision had changed his entire life. Unfortunately for him and many others, there was no way out. The A.U.C. was far too powerful.

He had heard stories of men trying to escape to other countries with Narco money and vividly remembered seeing the man stabbed to death inside the Finca. "Yes, sir. Where will I be transporting the cargo?" he asked gravely.

"You will arrive in Honduras and travel up the coast to Guatemala where you will collect the payment. One of the first mates went missing and, since you're the only transporter with experience on the water, we have chosen you for the opportunity." *Opportunity, my ass.* "Be very careful, Marco, those smugglers up there are just as dangerous as the jungles they live in. You will have protection from the Hondurans; they are reliable men we have worked with in the past. Essentially, you are to ensure we receive the correct payment, to the exact dollar, and that the shipment arrives as scheduled."

"So I'm going to be transporting cocaine to Guatemala, where I will be receiving cash to bring back here?"

"Exactly, Niño. But out there the code for cocaine is flores, so don't let them hear you say its real name."

Marco nodded and stared out the window, wrestling with the idea of shooting Oso, jumping out of the truck, and making a run for it. He knew that was unrealistic—he would be caught immediately—and he couldn't bring himself to shoot Oso. Marco refused to believe he had become that kind of person.

They ultimately pulled up to the gates of the Finca and drove to boat docks, where the forty-two-foot speedboats were waiting. He was very grateful, at that moment, that his parents had taken him to the ocean so many times as a child and that he had become a natural swimmer for he had no idea what would await him when he got on that boat.

The men loaded up the product, two thousand kilos of cocaine. "What's all this worth?" Marco asked.

"With each kilo being worth twenty thousand dollars, the whole shipment has a street value of forty million dollars in LA and Miami. In New York City it can be as high as a hundred million. Expect no less than twenty million dollars from the Guatemalans. We sell it to them wholesale and let them deal with the Americans. That's the deal this time."

Food and water were loaded on the boat as well. The boat had a captain, two auxiliary sailors, a trusted product protector, Marco, and a mechanic who watched to make sure the engines functioned properly and was able to repair them if anything went awry.

The captain spoke to Marco once everything had been packed and loaded. "Here is the rundown. We have an eighteen-hour trip ahead of us. The only time we will stop is to drink some water and eat for about twenty minutes. The rest of the time we will be going full throttle at about thirty-nine knots. There are five motors. In the event that one goes out, our mechanic will fix it and we have support boats we can contact if necessary, so do not worry. The most important thing is to stay calm. Even if you get sick, we cannot stop. It's very important we make it on time. If you need anything, let me know."

Marco nodded and mumbled, "Thanks."

Marco was making his way up the dock, to jump on the boat, when Oso called his name.

"Yeah, boss?" Marco said as Oso caught up with him.

"Take this," the bear-sized man said. Oso handed Marco what looked like a sheathed knife. He pulled a black eight-inch steel blade with serrated edges from the leather casing. It looked lethal and sharp. "It belonged to my son," Oso said softly, looking at Marco. "I hope you don't have to use it."

"Your son?"

"Yes, my son," Oso said sadly. "His name was Diego, he was about your age when he was killed. So make sure you come back in one piece, we need you around here."

Oso's genuine gesture had humbled Marco. He had never expected such confidence from the bear-sized man. "Gracias, Oso." Marco put the sheath in his waistband opposite his pistol.

"*A la orden*, Niño, safe travels," he replied with a soft smile before turning and leaving the dock. Marco smiled and watched his friend walk away before hopping onto the boat and making his way to the back, overlooking the vast blue sea.

Eighteen hours on a full-throttle speedboat. This is going to suck. And it did. The captain had not been lying. After Marco said his goodbyes to Oso and grabbed his bag, the boat disembarked on its journey. The roaring engines made it impossible to talk or sleep. Every time the boat hit a big wave, it came down hard on the water, shaking the whole boat. Marco found a spot in the corner and did his best to strap himself down. He stared at the Colombian shore as it grew smaller and smaller. He had never left Colombia and had NEVER envisioned that his would be how his first trip abroad would be.

Time passed as he gazed out at the ocean. Day turned to night and the boat finally began to slow down. The captain said something into his radio, but it sounded like gibberish. A little while later another boat appeared in the distance. Marco began to think the worst, but one look at the smiling captain and he felt better.

"OK, guys, twenty minutes." The men quickly grabbed food and water out of bags and began to devour them. The ham and cheese sandwiches were a welcome relief to the sailors' aching bellies after their long travel overseas.

The other boat encroached on them and then pulled up beside them. The sailors began to pump fuel into their boat from the other vessel. "Where are we?" Marco asked the captain.

"In Altamar. They have a fuel boat ready for us so we can go quickly. It's a fishing boat contracted by The Patron."

"How do they know were here?" Marco asked.

"We meet up using GPS coordinates. We have an entire code for it. For example 'Carolina' would be code for 'thirty-one.' 'C,' because it's the third letter in the alphabet, means 'three' and 'A,' because it's the first, means 'one.' Resulting in thirty-one. *Estoy en Carolina enfrentre de su casa* means 'I'm at the point.' That's why the military can never figure out where we are. They can't decrypt our messages."

Marco was amazed. He hadn't realized the complexity of the operation. *Impressive.*

"What happens if we don't get the cocaine there?" Marco asked.

The captain looked at him and any joy his face had previously held had vanished. "First, call it flores, second, that would be very bad for us, Niño, but if you really want to know I will tell you a story."

Marco nodded.

"Very well," he said sharply. "I had a friend who was also a ship captain. He had successfully done about ten trips and had about three million dollars to his name. A small fortune if I may say so myself. He had a sister and a cousin he took with him on a trip. Because the seas were stormy, he had to go to a safe and secret spot, a rock cave, where he stored the cocaine. While he was resting, his sister and cousin robbed him of five hundred kilos. When the supervisor counted he saw that five hundred kilos were missing and informed my friend. He realized what had happened after his sister and cousin had disappeared. The captain told Carlos Castano himself that he was going to make up the money he had been robbed of with work. Castano agreed and told the captain he could not leave the Finca, other than for his shipments, until he had been paid back in full.

"At the time the U.S. Navy was just starting to become more involved in their 'drug war,' and it became increasingly difficult to move product. Radar was becoming more popular and US ships were within two hundred miles of San Andreas. Airplanes were and still are being used. In order for the captain to continue working, he had to be more careful and somehow double his trips.

"He had his brother, Juanci, who was also a captain, help him do shipments to cut the repayment time in half.

Juanci agreed because he wanted to save his brother's life, but he wanted to know where his brother was and that he was safe. El Patron said he was in the Finca and he'd have him back when the debt was repaid. Each of them took different routes. After months, Juanci calculated that the debt had been repaid, and he asked for his brother back." The captain let out a deep sigh before continuing.

"One day Juanci arrived home and found his mother on the floor. She had opened a package, meant for him, from El Patron. That package contained the head of his brother and his clothes. His mother had opened the box and suffered a heart attack upon seeing the dismembered head of her eldest son. Juanci, who worked for the Cali Cartel, wanted vengeance. The Cali Cartel said they could do nothing because his brother had stolen and that was Narco law: if you steal, you die. At the time they didn't know it was his sister and cousin who were the real thieves. They didn't believe his story.

"The A.U.C. sent someone out to San Andreas to investigate how the product had been stolen and to prevent further losses. Their investigator found out that his sister and cousin were selling the cocaine on the beach for a hundred fifty dollars for a kilo. Basically giving it away, and it was them who had stolen it, not the captain. One of the men who had slashed the head off my friend found the sister, raped her, and then told her what he had done because of her theft. He's sick in the head and she is lucky to be alive.

"They later found the cousin and buried him headfirst in the sand, suffocating him to death. The dealers on the island of San Andres began giving back the product because they didn't want to die. The cartel recovered three hundred fifty of the original five hundred kilos of cocaine. It was awful for the island. It was a small town and a lot of people died. That, Niño, is what will happen if we do not successfully deliver this product." The captain looked emotionally drained from telling the story and ran his fingers through his hair.

Marco believed it. These men were ruthless. Who knew what other awful things they had done? He vowed he would do everything he could to make sure this product made it. His life depended on it.

CHAPTER TEN

HONDURAS

It was nearing twilight when the boat approached the coast of Honduras. The sun was setting, giving the jungle terrain and ocean water a beautiful orange and yellow glow. But Marco knew the beauty was to be short lived for, as the sun went down, darkness would soon creep upon them, bringing with it all sorts of dangers. The captain began diminishing speed as they got closer to the poorly made wooden harbor to dock. The anchorage looked like it could splinter and break apart any second. One of the sailors tied the rope around the side staffs and pulled the boat parallel to the dock, securing them in place. The captain disembarked and signaled for Marco to follow him. A small dark man came to meet them. *"Bien venido a Honduras."* Marco felt he was safe in assuming the man was from Honduras as he had on a Honduran national team soccer jersey.

"We are looking for Fernando," the captain said.

"Fernando? Who would be looking for a loser like that?" The Honduran patted his big stomach.

"I would be careful who you insult."

The man let out a boisterous laugh. "Foolish Colombians, you are almost as dumb as you are bad at soccer. I am Fernando." He whistled and a moment later

Marco heard an engine rumbling and brush being shuffled in the forest. "We will pull up the trucks and help you unload," Fernando said with a smile.

The Hondurans pulled up in a massive military truck. Eight Honduran men filed out from behind the truck. It was a mix of tall and skinny and short and strong. *What a group,* thought Marco. All the men, Colombian and Honduran, formed an assembly line to accelerate the unloading process. One by one, each bag of cocaine was loaded up onto the truck. "What now?" Marco asked the captain.

"Now you accompany these men to make sure everything goes smoothly. If you are not back in a couple of days, we will assume you're dead."

"Great." Marco rolled his eyes.

"Niño, you need to be sharp out there, this is no joking matter," the captain said sternly, glaring at him. Marco looked at the heavy jungle and gave a silent prayer.

Two more Jeeps appeared from the jungle. The Honduran men that had just helped the Colombian crew unload a boat filled them. Marco could see these men were armed to the teeth. He saw AK-47s, AR-15s, and M16s. It was like they had a few of every assault rifle ever made. It made the pistol on Marco's waistband feel a bit puny.

"Hop into the truck, Niño. These men will watch your front and back throughout the trip. You will be driving up the coast until you reach San Pedro. It takes a few hours because the roads are dark and very dense with brush. Good luck. I will see you soon." They shook hands and Marco made his way toward the passenger side of the truck. He stopped in front of the door and looked at the handle and then at his guards. He felt very uneasy entrusting his life to a bunch of men he did not know, but what other choice did he truly have? He hopped in and soon they were on their way.

One of the Jeeps had taken position in front of the truck and the other behind. Each one was filled with the heavily armed men on high alert. *I hope the safeties are on or they might accidently shoot each other.* After they had driven for a couple of minutes, the brush opened up, revealing an area similar to the one in the Colombian Finca but much smaller. The Hondurans were producing their own cocaine from what Marco could tell by looking at the open stations. It was obvious the operation was nowhere near the size of his cartels.

"We do what we can here." Fernando had been watching Marco's eyes take everything in. "Out here the brush is too much. We do much more inland, the coast is mostly for transporting. Money is money, ya know."

Marco nodded and looked out the window once again, not feeling very eager to make small talk. He noticed a shirtless man sitting on what looked like a wooden plank. It was a very small board, maybe one foot by one foot. It was just big enough to sit on. He was hugging the pole the board clung to, with his arms and legs, in an effort to avoid falling down. Below him there was a pit, but from his angle Marco could not see into it. "What is that?" Marco asked Fernando.

The Honduran gave a snorting laugh and said, "That's the crocodile pit, there are many ways to kill a man but crocodiles are especially terrifying. They snap down on you with those huge jaws and it's impossible to get back out. Then they roll around until they have twisted and broken your limbs. Then they drown you. They'll bring you down with them until you're doing nothing but swallowing water, and if they're not hungry they'll just leave you there to rot and come back for you later when they are." Marco's jaw dropped and his eyes widened. He felt like he had seen it all, but this was truly horrifying.

He looked at the man on the pole and could see that the skin on his back was peeling. "How long has he been there?"

"A few days," the driver said. "He's a snitch, he will die there. Someone may give him mercy and just shoot him, or he will starve, pass out, and then fall into the pit, *a la muerte*, to the death." Marco forced his eyes away and leaned back into his seat, grateful to not be that guy. "You are still young, Niño, there are worse ways to die than that. I hope you are spared from witnessing it but you probably will."

There was no more talking after that. Marco would be very happy to never see this man again and did everything he could to occupy his mind with anything other than death as they rode on toward San Pedro. Being a transporter wasn't so bad compared to what the man on the pole was experiencing. *What a perspective.*

It was a rough ride; the truck rattled over the bumpy dirt road throughout the trip. Darkness soon fell on them like a blanket, bringing its own hazards. They seemed to be surrounded by jungle, and Marco definitely had no idea where they were and was becoming irritated at all the mosquitoes that had decided he would be a delicious dinner. Slowly the minutes ticked by, one by one.

Ultimately, the jungle gave way. Marco looked at the digital clock on the dashboard; it was 2:00 a.m. He had not slept well in days, and sleep was creeping up on him. But every time he was within seconds of having a snooze, the truck rolled over a pothole, causing his head to bump against the window, or a foreign sound invaded his ears, pumping adrenaline through his body and keeping him alert. Sleep would have been impossible even without those distractions as Fernando incessantly whistled. Marco pulled out the knife Oso had given him and noticed a small pouch on the outside of the leather sheath. He unbuttoned the pouch, revealing a small black sharpening stone. Marco decided to put his time to use and began sharpening his new knife.

He glanced up some time later and saw a sign that said "Bienvenido a San Pedro." The streets were completely empty and very dark. All of the shops had iron bars in front of the entrances and windows. There was only one streetlight that was operational and, on occasion, it flickered in and out. The caravan moved smoothly through the city, undisturbed, until a couple of cars emerged from the darkness on either side of them. When they got closer he saw it was the police.

Marco drew in a sharp breath and gripped the handle of his pistol with a force that would crush most glass. He was not going to jail in Honduras without a fight; he knew that much. Marco looked over at Fernando, who didn't seem to be alarmed. The policeman shouted for them to stop. Two officers spilled out of each of the cars. All of them were short, stout men with short hair. They walked around the truck, scanning it up and down with puffed chests, and approached the driver's door.

"Buenos dias, senor," Fernando said.

"What are you doing here? At this hour?" the officer said sternly.

"Bringing a shipment of potatoes."

"The disrespect you have bringing your garbage through our streets," the officer said with venom in his words.

"I am sure we can come to a civil agreement, senor, we will pay for the privilege." Fernando was calm as one could be.

"Who do you think we are? Peruvians? Get out of the truck!" He put his hand on his holstered pistol. The truck driver honked twice and, like lightning, all the Hondurans hopped out of their Jeeps with their assault rifles pointed directly at the officers. Clicks could be heard as each man readied his gun for fire. The four officers who had been so brave a moment ago immediately raised their hands above their heads. They were surrounded and severely outnumbered. "Bueno, amigo," Fernando said. "Here is five hundred dollars for each of you." Fernando pulled out a wad of cash and waved it in front of the officer. "What will it be, amigo? *Plata o plomo*?"

"Thank you for your generosity, senor. Have a safe trip." The officers reached for the money and slowly walked backward to their cars, arms still raised.

The men continued to point their weapons at the officers until they had driven into the darkness. "Bueno, let's go!" Fernando banged the side of his door. The men hopped back into their trucks and continued their trip up the Honduran coast to Guatemala. *There's even less rules here than in Colombia.*

CHAPTER ELEVEN

GUATEMALA

As the sun rose, the hot and bumpy ride grew tiring. The only activity Marco could see outside of the window was a couple of stray dogs rummaging through the garbage. It had been too dark once they drove out of San Pedro to see anything until the sun came up. The brush surrounding the trail was so thick that branches and leaves were constantly scraping against the truck. "How much longer?" Marco asked Fernando. "We are almost there. Less than an hour," he replied, obviously becoming weary of the journey as well.

The next few miles seemed to drag on forever, but they finally arrived. They pulled into a clearing, and he saw some cars and a truck waiting for them. Beside them stood the Guatemalans. Marco counted sixteen of them of all shapes and sizes. Each one carried a machine gun. Marco and the Hondurans pulled up to them. "Buenas tardes, senores," Fernando said to the Guatemalans. "Let's do this smoothly and quickly."

Marco continued to eye the Guatemalans' firepower, knowing full well they were outnumbered two to one. He really hoped it wouldn't come to that as he knew it wouldn't end well for anyone. The Guatemalans began to bring out briefcases of money, and Fernando instructed his men to take out the cocaine. Once each party had taken out their supply, the Guatemalans started weighing the cocaine-filled packages as well as testing the quality of the drug. Marco got out of the car and started counting the money.

Marco yearned to eyeball it and leave immediately, but he didn't dare. He needed to be sure. He didn't want to end up being decapitated like the captain's friend. He almost lost track a few times because bugs kept stinging him, distracting him from his duties, but eventually he was very pleased to see it was all there, twenty million dollars, all in hundred-dollar bills. It was more money than Marco had ever seen in one place. *Thank God*, he thought, relaxing just a bit. Marco had no idea what he would do if there were some missing. He didn't want to imagine what would have happened to him or the Guatemalans if there were. Once Marco had counted the money, he gave Fernando a nod and a thumbs up. The Honduran Patron ordered his men to pack the cash into the truck. It was time to go home and nightfall was rapidly approaching.

The driver shook hands with the Guatemalan sicarios and said goodbye. Once Marco and the Hondurans were driving back with the money safely in hand, Marco gave a huge sigh of relief. *In hindsight I need to get a bigger gun. This little pistol would be like a water gun compared to the fury of lead those machine guns could lay down.*

His thoughts were cut short as he heard engines approaching. He leaned out the window and looked around. Leaves from the nearby brush smacked him on the head. It sounded like several small engines, like a mob of wasps enclosing on them. Marco peered into the darkness to inspect the foreign sound and was met with gunfire. A bullet flew by his ear, barely missing him and taking the side-view mirror with it. "Ahh!" Marco pulled his head back into the truck and looked at the broken side-view mirror. More bullets began to fly. Someone was firing at them from behind. It was the Guatemalans.

With all of the screams and shouts in Spanish, everything seemed to slow down for Marco. The only things visible through the darkness were the flashes emanating from enemy barrels as they fired at Marco and his crew. "FIRE!" one of the Hondurans screamed as they shot back roaring blasts, discharging bullets in the darkness in every direction.

Marco could hear screams as men from both sides were mowed down. The attackers were closing in on them. The Guatemalans on dirt bikes and ATVs were chasing them down, no doubt wanting to double up on their profit and get their money back.

A hard thump and a load groan were heard as one of the bikes lost control in the brush and smashed into the ground, causing a wheel to break off and roll away. Marco heard a nearby engine roar and the rustling of branches as another dirt bike maneuvered its way parallel to him. As the biker's gunner reloaded, Marco pulled out his pistol and shot furiously at the Guatemalans, screaming *"HIJO DE PUTA!"* with every pull of the trigger. He hit the bike's driver and watched as he skidded directly into a tree, generating a loud crash. "STOP THE TRUCK!" Marco roared.

As Fernando stopped, Marco heard them buzzing past them on either side. He jumped out of the passenger side and ran to the back of the truck. Most of his men had been shot, but only one lay dead. He turned to address the men in the trucks as well. "Hide in the brush! When they come back mow those motherfuckers down!"

The men moved. The buzzing stopped. For a moment everything was silent. Marco dove into the brush to find cover. In the distance the Guatemalans had jumped off their vehicles, and their footsteps could be heard as they moved on foot over the vegetation.

His heart was pounding, his breathing was heavy, and sweat was dripping down his forehead. He lay in the dirt and used the bushes as camouflage. He moved the leaves with the barrel of his pistol, aiming forward. All he could hear was his own breathing and his heart racing. His eyes were adjusting to the darkness and his ears to silence. He could hear movement ahead and undecipherable whispers. He focused his eyes in the direction he heard footsteps. Black silhouettes in the distance began to emerge, moving slowly. Then they stopped, dropping low to the ground. Undoubtedly they were looking for their prey.

The adrenaline was pumping through Marcos's veins. He had never been more alert in his life. Marco carefully aimed at his attackers, making sure not to lose sight of them. They began to move again, slowly creeping forward, becoming larger targets. *It's them or me*, he thought as he pulled the trigger. His comrades began to fire as well, unleashing hell on earth toward their assailants. The area which, just a second ago, had been dark and silent was filled with the flashing of gunfire, the screams of men, and the rattling of machine guns. There was a barrage of bullets, and every dark distant figure dropped to the earth, never to make another sound or breathe another breath.

Panting for air, Marco rolled over onto his back. He was lucky to be alive. All he could think of was his family, and how he had been inches away from never seeing them again. He took a few deep breaths and then slowly stood up. "It's all clear," one of the men said, and they all gathered near the truck.

Walking back toward the passenger's side, he stopped at the back of the truck. He saw two lifeless bodies. *Two men that will never see their families again, two families that will never again be whole.* As his adrenaline level came down, Marco began to feel desolate. *These men didn't have to die. But they did and for what? Money? Drugs?*

Fernando came to Marco's side and put his hand on his shoulder. "They were good men, friends of mine since childhood," he said with tears in his eyes. "Good husbands and better fathers."

"What will happen to them?" Marco asked.

"We will bury them and their families will be taken care of by The Patron, that's Narco law. Believe it or not, one day each one of us one will stop breathing, turn cold, and die. That's the way of the world." Everyone gave the dead their soundless respects before Fernando broke the silence whispering, "Let's go."

The men jumped into the back of the truck, exhausted. Marco's sadness had turned into nothing; he felt completely numb as he leaned against the truck. He forced his body into action and moved into the passenger seat, laying his head on the side door. Silent tears rolled down his cheeks. He felt like he was slowly dying, or that it was only a matter of time until he did, but he did not want to die. There was so much he had not done; he had too much to live for.

CHAPTER TWELVE

PAYDAY

Marco awoke with a slam. The truck hit a pothole, causing his head to bang against the side door. "Ow!" He held his fingers to the wound, making sure he hadn't drawn blood. The sun had started to rise, and rays were beginning to flood the jungle with light. Looking to the horizon he could see the almost mystic glow of the orange sun. It was a beautiful sunrise, to say the least, but Marco didn't have time to take in the moment as the events of the prior night began to flood his mind.

He looked at his pistol, which was completely empty for the first time since he had held it. He didn't know whether it was his bullets or his men's that had killed his attackers, but he didn't really care. He was alive and that was the only thing that mattered to him.

He heard a buzzing in the distance as Fernando began to slow down in the middle of the jungle. The two Jeeps did the same. Everything went quiet as the Hondurans turned off their engines. The buzzing grew louder and louder. The driver poked his head out of the window and looked up. He turned back to Marco and put his finger to his lips. The buzzing continued to grow louder and could be heard behind him. Marco tried to look behind them using the non-existent side-view mirror, forgetting that it had been shot off the night before. He poked his head out of the window and looked up just as the driver had done. He saw a jet encroaching on their location. It was going to fly right over them. Marco held his breath as the jet zoomed by them.

Once the plane was no longer visible, Fernando restarted the engine and continued forward. "Fucking gringos, man," he said to Marco. "We do some bad shit but they'll stick you in a cage forever, to me that's worse than death."

As hours passed by, the truck returned to the clearing near the beach where Marco's Central American journey had begun. Everything had remained the same except for one thing. There no longer was a man hugging a pole over a pit. The plank was vacant. Marco tried to distract himself from the memory by sharpening his knife. But with every swipe he could only hear the crunch of the crocodile snapping its powerful jaws on the man's body. Another swipe, another chomp. With the last swipe he envisioned the man with his lungs full of water, drowned at the bottom of the pit. Marco shuddered at the unknown man's brutal fate

Once out of the clearing Marco silently pumped his fist as he saw the captain was still there waiting for them on the boat. Few words were said while Marco and the remaining men moved the money from the truck to the boat. One look at Marco and the Hondurans, and the Colombians knew all they needed to know. They had the good sense not to ask. Marco was ready to be back in Colombia. "We're going back to the Finca, right?" an exhausted Marco asked the captain.

"Yes," was the captain's entire response.

Marco nodded and went to say his goodbyes to the Hondurans before boarding and making himself comfortable at the front of the boat. He knew he couldn't sit there and mope around. He had to be strong and brave; he was a Narco.

The mechanic sat down next to Marco. He was a handsome man with green eyes and a friendly smile. "Hola, the name's Giovanni, but you can call me Gio."

"Hey Gio, I'm Marco." They both looked out onto the water.

"It's a pretty crazy life we live, man, I can only imagine what happened last night, you look kinda beat up," Gio said. Marco was once again covered in dirt and had scratches on his arms and face from the brush. "The captain's got a really hard job too. Those damn gringos have been stepping shit up and tracking us down with some radar bullshit and making it near impossible to do our jobs. Did you see that plane? We would have been screwed if the jungle didn't cover everything up. It's a miracle they didn't see the boat. Who do they think they are?"

"What do you mean?" Marco asked.

"America, man," he said lighting a cigarette. He offered one to Marco and he accepted. *It's been a long week,* he thought.

"Those gringos are spending billions of dollars for this white shit, and Uncle Sam wants his cut. It's crazy, man," Gio continued. "If I had extra cash lying around like that, I'd do something with it. Feed my kids, build a school, maybe even send them to college. Shit, half the time we don't have power or water, and they want to lock us up for making a decent living. They're full of shit, too. They'll lie to you, saying they're gonna help you, but all they really want is to get their piece, damn liars. Rather than love, money, faith, fame, and fairness, give me truth, man. Every human deserves at least that. I bet they put their boots on the ground too one day when they've lubed up our government enough."

Marco took one last drag of his cigarette and flicked it into the ocean. "It's beautiful," he said softly, not having the energy to talk politics.

"What?"

"The ocean, man, it's so peaceful and blue. It's massive, I can't even see to the other side. I used to go a lot with my family when I was little. I have always felt at peace on the water."

Gio smiled at Marco and chuckled. "Just wait till you have to sail through a storm, my friend, that shit is terrifying. One wave can come over the side of the ship and take you under. The ocean deserves our respect as well as our admiration."

"Yeah, you're right," Marco said. "How long have you been doing this?"

"Too long, my friend, way too long."

The rest of the trip went smoothly as Marco chatted and got to know the other gentlemen. He really started to feel like he belonged. He had gained their respect as they were all impressed with the previous night's story. It was a cool sensation. *The ride back passed much faster than the ride there*, he thought as Colombia came into view.

He smiled at the thought of being on his home soil and of returning to Catalina. *There really is no place like home.*

When the boat docked Marco hopped onto the beach. He had never been so happy to have sand between his toes. He took a moment to appreciate being home and then began helping the men move the money off the boat and onto the beach for transport. Marco looked up and saw Oso standing next to two white men wearing exquisite white suits and sunglasses.

Oso saw Marco and waved him over. "Marco, meet Los Velasco."

Marco shook their hands and introduced himself.

"They're from Argentina, they clean all our money. All those bags of cash you transport are washed through their businesses in Bogota. For a nice cut of the pie, of course." Oso grinned.

The taller of the two said, "Nice to meet you, young man" He was blonde and handsome and had a stunning smile. The second was wearing a white fedora and smoking a cigar. Both wore gold watches and rings.

"What are your businesses?" Marco asked, knowing people loved talking about their success.

"An entertainment business in Bogota," the one smoking a cigar said between puffs.

"How much do you launder?" Marco asked.

"I would rather not say," he replied, smiling and taking another puff of his cigar.

"Marco is one of our youngest and most promising," Oso interjected. "No need to worry, Velasco." Oso ruffled

Marco's hair. "OK, Marco, let's go. Let's let these gentlemen do their jobs. I am sure you want some rest."

Marco gratefully nodded and followed Oso to his truck.

"OK, give me the lowdown. How did it go?"

Marco sighed and told him the whole story as they drove through the Finca to his apartment. Nothing much had changed. The Finca was as lively as ever. He even saw children stepping on the coca leaves to prepare them for production.

Once Marco had finished his story, Oso put his hand on his shoulder. "I'm glad you're OK, kid. It's a rough life we live, but in this country it's the only chance we have. If you need anything just call me. You're family now, the A.U.C. is one. That's Narco law. Your friend Pitufo, by the way, has been doing a great job lately, but he has been spending a lot of money. I need you to look into that while you're back, make sure he is not bending any rules. You will resume your normal transport duties until we need you otherwise."

Oso pulled up to Marco's beach apartment. "Get some rest, my friend. You've earned it. Oh, and here is your cut." Oso reached into the backseat of the truck and threw him a duffle bag. Marco unzipped it a bit and saw it was full of cash. "Wow," he said, his jaw dropping. "How much is this?"

"A million dollars. Leave it in your house. Banks will ask questions. Keep it cash. Don't draw attention to yourself. Maybe now you'll understand why we do it." He smiled. "It's the perfect product, baby, it creates demand for itself. As long as those gringos keep snorting it, we'll keep making it and shipping it. Adios, Niño." Oso tore up the gravel, as he left the complex, sending tiny rocks and dirt everywhere.

Marco could not believe his new wealth. His stomach filled with so much excitement he didn't know what to do with it. He quickly went into the safety of his apartment. He hoped his guards would arrive soon; he really needed them now.

He tossed the bag onto his bed and unzipped it, pulling out wads of cash. He could not help but smile. He took the rubber band off one of the wads and tossed the roll of cash into the air, letting money rain back down on top of him. For the first time in a long time, he felt very happy. This was more money than most people earned their whole lives, and he had made it in just a few days. *This isn't so bad.* The exhaustion of the previous days quickly rushed back and he lay down on his money-covered bed to get some well-deserved sleep.

CHAPTER THIRTEEN

EL PATAN

Marco awoke the next morning, and some of his money stuck to his face as he lifted his head. He resolved to pick up the cash after a shower. It felt amazing to be back in his apartment, mostly because he finally felt safe and there were no bugs. They had eaten him alive in the jungle. After a long hot shower he was famished, so he went into the kitchen. There was no food in the fridge. He would have to go get some. He closed the fridge and noticed a note taped to it. It read:

My love,

I know you will never read this but I can now mark a before and after you.

Before you, I didn't believe you could find love without searching for it.

Before you, I didn't believe anymore that someone could make you happy with just a smile.

Before you, I didn't believe there was someone that would listen to me.

Before you, I didn't believe there were men that knew how to treat a lady.

Before you, I didn't believe someone could take care of you like you were the most valuable thing on the planet.

Before you, I didn't believe someone could kiss me so beautifully and sincerely. I loved you by accident because in that moment the last thing I thought about was falling in love. Without a doubt those loves are the best ones.

I will never try to forget you and even if I did try I would fail.

I loved seeing you and making you mine with just a glance.

I adored your lips and your chest is my paradise.

I loved you and believed we were meant to be.

Te amo,

Catalina Martinez

Marco's heart was full of anguish at finishing the letter. He felt guilty for having abandoned Catalina. He had hoped that she would be here awaiting his return, and he couldn't understand why she had left. "I know you will never read this!? What does that even mean!?" They had spent nights discussing the possibility that he may be forced to leave, but he had always promised to return. He was angry, hurt, and confused all at once. It was an unbearable tornado of emotion. He sat down with his back to the refrigerator and his head in his hands.

He would miss her sweet vanilla scent and the way her lips tasted like coffee in the morning. He longed to hold her and caress her silky dark hair while staring into her unforgettable emerald green eyes. He yearned to kiss her on the forehead in the most innocent of ways. She was his queen and he had left her without a king. He prayed that the universe kept her safe and that, at some point on the long, winding, obstacle-filled road we call life, he would find her and, God willing, they could pick up where they had left off.

Bang, Bang. A loud knock on the door broke Marco's romantic fantasy and dragged him back down to his dangerous reality. "Who is it?" he shouted with a hoarse voice.

"It's Pitufo, faggot, open the door." Marco grinned and let him in. Pitufo took a seat on Marco's couch. He still looked like a rat, albeit a very exquisite rat. He was wearing a massive gold watch, gold chain, diamond earrings, and the highest end clothing you could buy in Colombia.

"Looking good, homie, you been blowing all your cash on clothes?"

"Yeah, clothes, whores, and I got myself a sweet new motorcycle and a truck. Oso told me you were back and had a hell of a trip, you ready to get back to work?"

"Yeah, making money is kind of addicting," Marco said with a laugh. "That's all your cash you're spending, right?"

"Of course." Pitufo avoided eye contact with Marco. Something was up, but Marco decided to wait until later to ask. "Wanna come to the Finca with me? I've got some business to discuss out there," Pitufo said.

"Yeah, I've got nothing to do. What's today anyway?"

"It's Sunday, God's day."

They both headed toward the door. Marco triple checked his locks and made sure everything was secure before heading toward the parking lot.

He was happy to see his bodyguards hanging out in the shade, looking as threatening as ever, drinking beers and smoking cigarettes. *Don't they want more out of life?* Marco thought as he waved at them. They walked up to Pitufo's new truck. It was nice, not as nice as Oso's but still really freaking nice. It was red and massive. They hopped in and the car shook as Pitufo turned the ignition and headed toward the Finca.

"Yo, you hear they let me bring my own guards from Medellin? I'm untouchable with these killers watching my back. They're the most dangerous sicarios in the world. We need to get a piece of that cash."

Marco said nothing, thinking about the bag of cash in his room and all the money he had just transported back from Honduras. He was already getting his piece. He was going to keep his head low, survive, and cash out.

"El Patron is going a little crazy too, keeps sending our guys out to fight those damn FARC guerillas. Those dudes are nuts. Trying to make the government socialist and shit, and the worst part is they're trying to get a piece of our market. That's not even mentioning the Americans. If they had their way, their army would be down here destroying everything we've built. I'm telling you, man, we just gotta get ours and get out. This country is going to shit."

"You've got a point," said Marco. "We gotta look out for ourselves."

"Exactly." Pitufo was happy to continue with this rant. Marco stared out the window. *Is there really a point in keeping on trying to do good? There is so much evil in the world. Why combat it? Why not just accept it and profit from it?*

The thought of his parents and Catalina hit him. A quote his father had once told him ran through his mind. "All the gods, all the heavens, and all the hells are within you." He was torn; he didn't know what to believe. The boys passed through the gates and passed the armed guards quickly. They were becoming more known and respected throughout the A.U.C. with each passing day.

The security had definitely been amped up as he saw more guards than ever before. Perhaps he had been too tired to notice the day before. They soon arrived at the main section by the beach. "All right, I'll be back in a little while, and we can go to a bar or something." Pitufo parked the truck and headed toward one of the makeshift houses. Marco looked around and saw Nico, one of the other transporter boys he had been in the house with a few months ago. He hopped out of the truck and followed Nico into a building.

It was dark, empty, and made of concrete. Once his eyes adjusted to the darkness, he was able to make out a figure lying on the ground. What Marco saw next was something he would never forget. There was a naked woman chained by her wrists. Standing nearby was a massive fat man with long dark greasy hair covering his eyes, a machete on his waist, and a flat piece of wood in his seemingly permanently dirty hand. When he got a closer look, Marco could see bruising and blood all across her body and in her hair, causing it to cling to her face.

Marco quickly walked over to Nico. "What the hell is happening?"

"DEA," Nico whispered. "It's confirmed but she won't admit it. She's claiming to be a Bolivian. It's a shame, really, she's a pretty woman."

"Who are you?" The man smacked her with the paddle. "Stop lying!"

"Who's that guy?" Marco asked Nico.

"That's El Patan, he's The Patron's muscle."

"My name is Lorena Garcia, I am a tourist from Bolivia!" the woman said, half sobbing.

"LIAR!" El Patan raised his hand high over his head before violently flogging the woman on her back. She screamed. Marco went numb. It was a disgusting sound. He pitied the woman and was scared for her safety, but he dared not intervene and risk his own life. El Patan seemed drunk off the power and control he had over the woman and was liable to take him out next.

"You were marked when you entered Colombia, Agent Rodriguez. Do you know what we pay for the heads of DEA agents here? Two hundred fifty thousand dollars. In Colombia you are a god with a quarter million dollars. So I think I will keep yours for myself." El Patan grabbed her by the hair and lifted her up, exposing her throat.

"No, PLEASE!" she screamed while trying to kick, scratch, and escape her captor to no avail. El Patan laughed a soulless laugh and raised his machete and, after one quick swing, held up her head while her body slammed lifelessly to the floor.

CHAPTER FOURTEEN

THE SUMMONING

As if someone had been choking him in his sleep, Marco awoke gasping for air. His sheets were covered in sweat and his mouth was especially parched. Months had passed since his trip to the gulf, witnessing the decapitation of the DEA agent, and Catalina's sudden departure. Sleeping had become difficult for him. He often had trouble quieting his mind to fall asleep and would consistently wake up in the middle of the night. But, from time to time, he could still hear her screams in his dreams. At times he would wake up in the middle of the night and think there were figures surrounding him. His mind was playing tricks on him. The things he had seen had had a profound impact on Marco. His view of the world was becoming more cynical, and he found himself caring less and less for others. His heart was hard and cold.

Financially speaking the last few months had been fruitful. Every week, he picked up half a million dollars to hold or deliver for The Patron. At one point he'd had twelve million dollars just sitting in his house. His extra bedroom was being used strictly to store money, and he was quickly running out of space. On occasion the boss would send one trusted guy to Marco's apartment to count the money and make sure everything was in order. Not a single dollar was ever missing from Marco's stash.

The A.U.C. continued to pay for the apartment and his other living expenses, so all of the money he made transporting was used for fun. He saved up enough money to buy an apartment in Cartagena for when he wanted a weekend getaway or a place to sleep after a delivery if he was too exhausted to drive back to Santa Marta. He also bought a beautiful thirty-eight-foot Baltic yacht to take out onto the water, for those adventurous cravings. He took it out for fishing trips and scuba diving and had legendary parties. The most beautiful women in all of Colombia had been there, in their bikinis, sipping champagne. He was the man. He had bought himself a new car, a brand-new black 2000 BMW, and wherever he went all the heads turned. He had also bought a new motorcycle, a CVR-900. He used his new bike for transporting. He could do his routes in ninety minutes with no traffic. He still loved the adrenaline the high speeds would give him.

He almost always had girls on the back, to avoid more attention, as he had done with Catalina. They put clothes in the suitcases to cover the money. If the cops ever pulled them over, they would look around, see the girl's panties, and say "move along." The girls were also prepared to perform special favors if a cop was especially strict and wouldn't accept a bribe, which usually worked. If things continued to get sour, he could outrun them on his bike. For the extra noble ones who could not be bought or ran from him, Marco always had his pistol loaded and at the ready, holstered behind his back, and his knife tied by his ankle. If he ever did get arrested, the A.U.C. would take care of him.

In Colombia, jail meant hookers, drinking, playing with your friends, and a short sentence for good behavior if you paid the right people. Extradition was the only thing Narcos really feared. In America no one gave a shit how much money you had or who you were. But this was Colombia. There wasn't anyone that couldn't be bought one way or another. That's the way it was. You looked out for you because no one else was.

It wasn't all cash, girls, and adrenaline. Lonely nights were becoming more common. Marco could not talk to his family; as far as they knew he had probably died. Almost two years had passed since he had left home. Marco resented having to ask his bosses for permission to do everything like they were his daddies. Marco was taken care of, but he knew it was because of the service he provided the A.U.C.; he understood he was expendable. If he defied them he would be severely punished. El Patron had to set the example and maintain the hierarchy. Marco and the other Niños were very rich, powerful, and ambitious. They were highly respected in the community, some would even say feared.

Tension in Colombia was beginning to escalate to unprecedented heights. There was a multifaceted battle being fought on three fronts. Wars were being declared between the cartels. The guerillas were moving further into the narcotics game, obtaining more market share and producing more cocaine to meet skyrocketing demand. Where there's easy money you're going to find a lot of players. The third was the government, who was cracking down hard on all the Narcos with the aid of the Americans. Shipments were being seized and the A.U.C. had to become increasingly creative on how to move their merchandise.

Anything you can think of was being exported with cocaine. Packages labeled tires, coffee, nuts, and even barrels filled with "toxic waste"—all of it was cocaine.

The increasing hostilities and government raids were driving Carlos Castano mad. El Patron had become increasingly violent, and people would often die for little or no reason. The boats began importing all kind of weapons from arms dealers, including pistols, assault rifles, grenades, and Humvees, to prepare for all-out war. It was a bloodcurdling time for Colombia and its people. Marco did his best to stay on The Patron's good side.

The violence and drug busts reduced supply, which had its upside for the A.U.C. It drove up price as demand continued to rise. There was blood money everywhere, and Marco was making sure to get his piece while laying low. The other Niños did the same, except Pitufo. He was spending a lot of money, more money than he could possibly have. Marco had begun to seriously worry about the consequences of his association with Pitufo. If his fears became a reality, it would be very bad for him and every other Niño. One afternoon as Marco was smoking a cigar on his balcony, looking at the sunset, pondering, and feeling especially adrift, there was a knock on his door.

Marco grabbed his pistol from the table next to him, walked toward the door, and looked out the peephole. It was one of his guards. Marco opened the door. "What's up?"

"El Patron called." He sounded uncharacteristically serious. "He wants you to go down to the Finca, he needs to talk to you."

"OK." Obediently, Marco grabbed his wallet off the countertop and headed toward his bike. He began taking deep breaths to calm his racing heart. Last minute summons were never good.

CHAPTER FIFTEEN

THE TOMB

The drive into the Finca was as usual. He waved to the guards as they opened the gate for him to drive through. The cooks were hard at work preparing the cocaine for packaging. Others weighed the product, some wrote down figures to keep track of production, and many more heavily armed men patrolled the perimeters. Marco got as far as his bike would take him and parked before continuing on foot.

The same young boys he'd played soccer with a couple of years ago were digging holes in the sand. *That feels like decades ago.* Sailors were preparing a boat for a shipment. He spotted Oso outside of one of the structures, and he waved Marco over. Marco flashed him a smile and said hello when he reached the building. Oso was stone faced and all business. "Inside, Marco," was all he said. *This can't be good.* The other Niños were all there already. Some sat against the wall, and others were standing, chatting, and smoking cigarettes. Marco leaned against a wall and lit one of his own. Time ticked by slowly as they all wondered why they had been summoned so abruptly.

Eventually, The Patron walked in with a heavy entourage of large heavily armed men, and Oso stood at his side. "AGAINST THE WALL!" one of the sicarios yelled.

"Woah, what's going on, amigo?" Nico dropped his cigarette and put it out with the heel of his shoe.

One of the men shot the ceiling. "NOW!" The Niños quickly obeyed. They got in a line against the far wall, across from The Patron and his men.

"You see these men, boys," The Patron began calmly. "They are my most loyal. They understand the Narco laws, they understand that without these laws we are just savages. There was a time when a man's word was everything. It saddens me to see that we no longer live in those times. Now, I could have my sicarios kill you but that would not solve anything. As you know our situation is becoming increasingly hostile and TRUST, gentlemen, is more important than ever. Now, one of you has broken that trust. Tell me who and no one dies. Don't tell me and all of you will die, it's very simple."

All of the Niños looked at each other with panic in their eyes. It was obvious none of them had any idea what was happening. Strangely, Marco realized he wasn't scared at all. He actually felt nothing. He had become so used to being a breath away from death that it had become a new normal. He no longer thought of what bad things could happen to him; he was no longer scared of life. Time continued to pass and none of the boys spoke.

"AHH, DAMN YOU ALL!" The Patron spat, losing his cool. *This is it,* Marco thought calmly, *I am going to die here and now.* The Patron walked up and down the row studying them all. "Fine, you don't want to talk, but you will. They always do. Take them to their pits." The Patron coated his words in venom. "HANDS ON YOUR HEADS, SPREAD APART!" one of the sicarios yelled, jamming his gun into

Pitufo's back. Once again the boys had no choice but to obey. "FILE OUT!"

The Niños were marched onto the beach at gunpoint. Daniel led the line followed by Marco, then Nico and, lastly, Pitufo. They reached an area about twenty yards from the brush and about forty yards from the shore. There had been four pits dug in a circle, each a little over five feet deep and nowhere near as wide. Each one was ordered into his respective pit, facing away from each other. Once inside the boys Marco had seen digging earlier appeared with shovels. Marco recognized the boy that walked in front of him and began pouring sand into his hole. It was the same boy who had been wearing the raggedy Miami Dolphins T-shirt; he had grown. The boy was avoiding eye contact with Marco at all costs. Each boy piled it in until each Niño was up to his throat in sand and unable to move. "We will see how long it takes for you to talk," said one of the sicarios as they left the Niños to rot in their sand tombs.

CHAPTER SIXTEEN

THE UNIVERSE

"This is straight up bullshit!" Daniel yelled.

"Yeah, which one of you bastards stole money!" Nico shouted.

"I didn't do it," said Pitufo in a high-pitched cracking voice. If they could have moved enough to look at Marco, they would have.

"Me either," said Marco earnestly. "Can that water get up here or what? Are we gonna drown?" Daniel eyed the rising tide.

"Nah, no way. They need us to move their money, they're not gonna kill us. Besides I don't think the tide comes this far up," said Nico, being his usual optimistic self.

"You're crazy if you think they won't kill us," Pitufo interjected. "They don't need us. There are a million starving guys that would love to take our spots."

"I've got sand in my ass," Nico said. "This sucks."

"Let's figure out a plan," Marco suggested.

"We can eat the sand and get out," said Daniel, humorously trying to bring down the tension.

"You're an idiot. I'm not eating any grainy ass sand," Pitufo said.

Marco could see the other Niños' heads wiggling around out of the corner of his eye and started to laugh. They looked like worms wiggling their way out of the ground.

"What are you laughing at, you idiot? We're trapped in sand and if we don't figure something out we are going to die here." Pitufo said.

"I say Pitufo takes the rap because he's the ugliest and he's probably got a tiny dick." Daniel laughed to himself.

"Fuck you, faggot, I bet you wanna see my dick," Pitufo replied.

"He would probably need a microscope," Nico retorted. The Niños couldn't help but laugh at this point except Pitufo, who continued to fume and struggle in a futile attempt to free himself.

The jokes soon went away as the inescapable reality loomed over them that they were unable to move. A few hours had passed and it was well past midnight. Marco could not really feel his toes and moving his legs was hopeless against the weight of the sand. Marco looked at the sand and studied each individual piece. Each grain was so small. Alone it was insignificant, not even noticeable. But combined with more sand, it had become his inescapable cage. The same sand he had been so happy to see when he returned from Honduras was the same entity currently entrapping him.

Occasional gusts of wind threw grains of sand into his face and mouth. Hours went by in silence as the rest of the boys tried to get some sleep. Marco's mind was racing as usual. So he entertained himself by staring at the stars. Rarely did he appreciate them the way they deserved to be treasured. The clouds had moved apart and he stared in awe. Thousands of stars covered the clear sky. It looked like freshly cut diamonds twinkling against black velvet. It was breathtaking. The sky was so big and the galaxy that lay beyond even bigger, full of stars, moons, suns. and who knew what else.

It made Marco feel small, very small. His ego had increased as much as his net worth had, but this situation was really putting his life in perspective. *In a universe as big as this one how much do my actions really matter?* Trapped in the sand, with nothing else to occupy his mind, he dwelled deeper in his thoughts. He wondered about life and death. *What is the point of it all? Has my existence ever made a small dent in the universe?* he asked himself. He knew the earth had begun spinning long before he arrived, and that it would continue to spin long after his last breath. *So what is the point? What is actually important?*

The only solid response he could conjure up was that of his family and of how much he missed them and loved them. His riches seemed insignificant now compared to the love he had felt when he was home. He would give every dollar back in order to return to his past peaceful life. *Love. That's the point. It has to be. Everyone does everything they do for love.* He thought of the men who had died in Honduras, selling narcotics so they could give better lives to their children, whom they loved. He thought of the women who inhaled toxic fumes while preparing the cocaine, so they could put food in their children's stomachs. *They did it for love.* He thought of his mother, who would always tell him to be home before dark, because she loved him. Marco had made up his mind. He was done with this Narco world. He would get out of this hellhole, get his freedom, and go home or die trying.

CHAPTER SEVENTEEN

GUARDIAN ANGEL

Marco awoke to the bright sunrise. The rays had disrupted his slumber. His face was itching so he tried to scratch it, but his arms wouldn't move. He opened his eyes and came crashing back to the reality of his present entrenched state. Unable to move he resolved not to struggle, to maintain his already dwindling energy. He was parched and he knew that, with the rising sun, the heat would rise and dehydration would become a problem.

His face was incredibly itchy, and he could feel the rest of his body irritating him as well. *Sand flies, damn sand flies.* He forced his face into all kinds of awkward contortions in an effort to alleviate the itching. The wind had blown sand into his hair, which began to drape over his eyes. He tried shaking his hair back in order to clear his vision. He saw a little crab dragging a shell in front of him and decided to blow at it to entertain himself. It instinctively jumped into its shell, prepared for the worst. *I wish I had a shell I could jump into.*

Unable to move Marco closed his eyes and tried to snooze to escape from his current situation. The sun had continued to rise, rapidly raising the temperature as well as his need for water. The sunrise was stunning, but it was far too difficult for Marco to appreciate any kind of beauty in his current situation. What seemed like hours passed as he busied himself studying the waves. It was melodic how the waves crashed into the shore and then so effortlessly found their way home as the surge pulled the water back into the ocean. *If I were water I could just move around this sand or soak it up.* None of the boys had said a word throughout the day, too thirsty and lethargic to speak.

The coolness of night made its presence known. He tried once again to escape, this time using his chin as a shovel. It was futile. Every time Marco moved, more sand would fall into its place. Marco heard all kinds of animal noises in the jungle and did his best to not let his mind wander to what would love to come and eat a few free meals. *I need water.* His mouth felt drier than sandpaper, and the sun was beginning to rise again. Swallowing was becoming difficult, and soon the sun was once again beaming down on him with full force. He could feel his skin burning. He could only imagine how cherry-like his face looked after back-to-back days boiling under the sun. His skin was feeling leathery and painful. He felt woozy as his breathing came in short shallow breaths. He was beginning to lose hope, and death by dehydration seemed imminent.

He heard a rustle behind him. He imagined the worst as he tried to turn his head. *It's a jaguar; it's going to maul my head.* "Who is it?" he exclaimed with a raspy voice. He heard another Niño grunt as he, once again, failed to free himself from his sand prison. He continued to struggle and contort his neck to see his attacker. The branches rustled even closer. The Niños all started grunting in an effort to dissuade the mysterious predator.

Marco heard a familiar giggle. "Relax, boys," he heard a girl say. "I'm not going to hurt you, in fact you are all probably going to love me." She circled around him and sat down in front of him, crossing her legs. It was Catalina. She was wearing a white dress and had a pack slung on one shoulder. She looked more gorgeous than ever. She had the same sun-kissed skin, long dark hair, and piercing green eyes and a smile that lit up Marco's world. "Are you an angel?" he asked thinking he was hallucinating.

She smiled even wider and let out an adorable laugh. "Ay mi amor, what have they done to you." She gently brushed sand off his face. "Here, I brought you water." She pulled a bottle out of her bag and unscrewed the cap. She gently brushed his hair out of his eyes and tipped the bottle up so Marco could take small sips. He was euphoric. It felt significantly better than the first chug of water after a long night of drinking.

"You are an angel," Marco said with a smile after finishing the bottle of water. She pulled out another bottle of water and a rag and began to gently wash off the grime that had accumulated on his face. Once he was clean she kissed him on the forehead. His heart fluttered. He had missed those lips so much. He couldn't believe what was happening.

"Here, I have this." She pulled out a black baseball cap and put it on Marco's head, giving him some more than welcome protection from the sun's relentless rays. *I never thought a piece of shade would bring me so much happiness.*

"Amor, what are you doing here, where have you been?" Marco asked weakly. Catalina's eyes began to tear up and Marco wished he could move his arms and embrace her. "I spoke to Oso and he told me my uncle had put you here, so I came immediately. I was so worried." Tears streamed down her face. "My uncle told me you had died in Central America, Marco. I was devastated. I'm so sorry I left. I should have waited, I'm so, so sorry. He can be such a cruel man." Tears would have sprung from Marco's eyes had he not been severely dehydrated.

"I've missed you so much, mi vida," Marco whispered, beyond grateful to have her sitting in front of him.

"Can we get some water too?" said Nico in a raspy voice. The others grunted in agreement.

"Yes, sorry, hold on, Marco." Catalina went around giving the Niños water before coming back around to him.

"Wait, who's your uncle?" Marco said, still woozy.

She sat down in front of him again. "Amor, my uncle is Carlos Castano."

"WHAT?! You never told me that."

She looked down and away from him and said softly, tears still running down her cheeks, "I never wanted it to affect us. I was scared you wouldn't want to be with me if you knew. It was safer if you didn't know. I tried to keep it from him too, but he somehow found out."

"I am so happy to see you, I couldn't care less about that. I am eternally grateful. You're saving our lives." Marco looked into her eyes and felt a powerful, inexplicable force. He couldn't take his eyes off of hers. It was more than her beauty. It was a whole world more than that.

"Why are you trapped in sand, Marco?" she asked, caressing his hair.

"I have no idea," he replied, his voice still raspy. "Well, that's not true, I know someone was stealing money from The Patron, but it was not me. I would never do that and I don't even know which one of the guys, if anyone, did." They heard voices in the distance and Catalina stood up.

"I have to leave, he would kill you immediately if he knew I did this. I will find out what I can. I will try to talk to him, mi vida. I'll bring you more water tomorrow and some food. I won't let you die, not again."

"Thank you, Catalina" Their eyes locked.

"*A la orden, carino,*" she whispered, giving him a wink, before walking back off into the bushes. Marco stared, once again, out into the ocean, bewildered but elated by what had just happened.

CHAPTER EIGHTEEN

SENTENCING

Night had fallen when Marco reopened his eyes. He heard a rustle in the bushes again and was slightly disappointed to see Oso appear this time. He was not alone. Half a dozen men came behind him. "That one," he directed, pointing to Pitufo. The men began to dig Pitufo out of his hole and, as soon as they could free him, four of them dragged him back toward camp. The remaining two began releasing Daniel and Nico.

"Marco!" Ban came to his side. "How are you feeling, little guy?"

"Awful," he whispered as he took inventory of his body's current state. His lips were cracking from dehydration and sun exposure. He could feel sun blisters protruding on his face. The sand fleas had not stopped their assault on his body, and he had sand in places he did not want to think about.

"Here's some water." Oso reached into his bag for a canteen before tipping it back, allowing Marco to take sips. "I have great news," he said while Marco drank. "For you, anyway. We found out who was stealing the money. It was Pitufo, that rat. So you are free to go, but first The Patron wants you to come back to the Finca."

"How did he find out?" Marco asked.

"Pitufo is an idiot. He tried to hire a sicario to kill Castano, and then he was going to make a break for it with the money he stole. But the sicario has been on Carlos's payroll in the past and knew who paid better and that he would pay even more handsomely for this information. Everyone has a price. We needed to know if the rest of you were purposefully withholding information from the A.U.C."

Once the canteen was empty, Oso began to dig Marco out of the sand with his hands.

"Wow, so what happens to me?" Marco asked.

"Nothing. You go back to work. Don't take it personal, Marco, it was just business."

Marco nodded but inside he knew that was impossible. He couldn't be treated worse than a misbehaving dog and just forget about it. What he had just experienced was inhumane.

"You look like shit," Oso said with a chuckle. "Where did you get this hat?" He burst into laughter. "Never mind that. Now let's get you out of there." Oso continued to use both hands to move massive heaps of sand away from Marco's body. Marco slowly felt the weight lessen as the sand gave way. He was soon able to move his shoulders enough to pull his arms out. His muscles were incredibly stiff. It felt unbelievably strange to move. Once he got feeling back, he used what little strength he had left to help free his lower body. Once they had dug to his lower thighs, he was able to wiggle his legs out and crawl onto the beach. He rolled onto his back and shook his legs until he could once again feel them. He was finally free from his sand cage.

"Do you have any more water, or food?" Marco asked Oso.

"What? No thank you so much, Oso, for releasing me?" Oso teased, obviously very happy to have Marco released. "I'm just kidding, yeah, I brought both but I suggest you wash off in the ocean first, you look and smell like crap." Marco gave a tiny chuckle.

"Thank you, Oso." Marco walked toward to the water, allowing his body to slowly come back to life. He got to the shoreline and dropped to his knees, allowing the water to wash him. The salt stung the wounds on his face but felt heavenly over the rest of his body. He just sat there for a moment as the water advanced and receded.

He needed food, lots of water, and a few good nights' sleep. He was almost done; he had to keep pushing past the exhaustion. *The hard part is over*, he repeated to himself. A wave came in and Marco stuck his head into it, allowing the water to slick his hair back and wash the sand out of it. He washed out his mouth with some salt water and headed back to shore, where Oso awaited him with water and sandwiches.

"Can we walk back to the Finca or do you need a minute?"

"I can walk, I'd rather walk, I haven't been able to in days." Marco devoured the sandwich and chugged the water as they walked back to the Finca. Oso led him into the same building where he had seen the DEA agent decapitated. The other Niños were already there, leaning against a wall, looking as miserable as Marco.

Pitufo was in the middle of the room, tied down to a metal table by his ankles and wrists, with a gag in his mouth.

All he could hear were muffled sobs. Soon The Patron walked in followed by El Patan, who was carrying a rusty saw.

At seeing the saw Pitufo went mad, like a bull trying to rid itself of its rider. He used every bit of strength he had to kick or pull the binds that tied him down but to no avail.

"You fool!" Castano hovered over the terrified Pitufo. "You broke Narco law. We gave you an opportunity and you stole from us. I spoke to your friends in Medellin; they wish you no sympathies. The A.U.C. is based on trust and you broke the cardinal rule. The air in your lungs belongs, TO ME! And now I will take what's mine, slowly, painfully." He motioned for El Patan to come over. "First his fingers, one at a time, then his hands and feet. Then move on to one arm and then the other, then each leg in turn, until he only has his head. Do it slowly. I want him to feel everything."

Pitufo was still struggling, with all his might, against his bindings and letting out gut-wrenching muffled screams. The Patron turned to the Niños and, in a calm collected manner, said, "I hope each of you learns from Pitufo's mistake, you may leave when El Patan is done. Also, we are going to cool it for a while. Everything's really hot right now, especially with the DEA. Keep the money in your apartments safe. When everything is calm we will get back to work. Think of it as a vacation. Keep out of trouble and we will contact you soon." El Patron walked out of the building.

El Patan let out a disturbing deep chuckle. He raised the saw and said, "Eenie, Meenie, Miney, Mo" between each of Pitufo's fingers, ultimately landing on the right pinky. He began sawing slowly. Pitufo began flailing, and his screams would have woken up the neighboring villages had he not been gagged.

Marco took off the hat Catalina had given him and used it to cover his eyes. He felt completely dead inside. But the sawing continued. There was no escaping the sound of blood dripping, bones splintering, and the gruesome sound emitted with each push and pull on the muscle. Pitufo lost his fingers and limbs one by one. Blood was spilling all over the floor. Once El Patan reached Pitufo's legs, Pitufo passed out from the pain. El Patan let out a disappointed groan. Pitufo wouldn't wake up. *What an awful way to spend your last few moments on earth.*

El Patan decided to cut his work short and finish by decapitating him. *He is definitely not waking up*, thought Marco, numb to the atrocities he had just witnessed. El Patan grabbed a spiked pole and shoved it inside Pitufo's lifeless head. Blood dripped down onto his hands and onto the floor. "Here, boy," he said to Nico, handing him Pitufo's head. "Put this at the front of the Finca so all will know what happens to those who steal from the Autodefensas Unidas de Colombia!"

CHAPTER NINETEEN

A NEW HOPE

Following his imprisonment, Marco slept for two whole days. The days following involved a lot of drinking and smoking. He took the other Niños out onto the boat to party. He spent the majority of his time trying to forget recent events and keep his mind occupied. He was on vacation, after all, and had more money than he knew what to do with, so he might as well enjoy himself. But once all the festivities ended, the laughing stopped. When it was dark and silent, Marco could hear Pitufo's muffled screaming.

Although he knew Pitufo had been wrong in stealing, he would not wish such a painful and ruthless death on anyone. It took a lot of alcohol to silence his mind. This allowed him to sleep. The other Niños seemed OK, or at least they pretended to be. He had not seen Catalina since she had brought him water and was busy searching for her throughout town. Needing something to occupy his time and mind, Marco bought some beachside land to build on. He paid in full, with cash.

He began to design and build a home he hoped to one day fill with a family. He wanted a house full of children's laughter and love. This new dream of his kept him going. Until it became a reality, at the very least he would have something to do. As the weeks passed Marco was torn between appreciating the simplicity of his current life and somewhat missing the adrenaline-filled life of a Narco. No word had been received concerning the cartel's plans for Marco and the Niños, only rumors that it was becoming increasingly difficult and expensive to transport cocaine as more and more shipments had been detained.

Marco was becoming increasingly fearful because he had heard El Patron had become very violent; people were dying for very little reason. He had started fighting the guerillas more fiercely. The FARC were looking for their piece of the pie. Marco began to think ahead, one day, as he was in town looking for more building supplies. He needed some tiles for the ocean-facing waterfall he wanted to build.

As he was daydreaming about what his future may contain, two gentle hands covered his eyes. "Guess who?" whispered a sweet voice behind him. Marco smiled. He would recognize that voice anywhere. He turned around and saw Catalina, who was smiling back at him, seducing him with her gorgeous green eyes.

"Hola, amor." Marco wrapped her up in a hug. "How are you?"

"I'm well, thank you. How are you feeling?" she replied sweetly.

"I'm good, just trying to keep busy. I actually have your hat at my house if you want to come get it. It was a life saver... well, I guess you were too," he said, smiling. "I really owe you. Can I make you dinner or something?"

"Girls don't like questions, Marco," she replied, playful as ever.

"OK, how about I'm making dinner tonight. Would you like to join me?"

"Still a question, sir"

Sir? I like that. "OK, fine, come over for dinner tonight."

"Sure, I'm kind of hungry now, though, so let's go get what we need and start cooking." They got some chicken, breadcrumbs, rice, and plantains and headed back to Marco's apartment.

"We're going to have pollo a la Manuela with coco rice," Marco said.

"What is pollo a la Manuela?"

"It's my grandmother's famous chicken recipe. You put the chicken in a pot until it cooks through. It's half pan-fried, half boiled. Once it's cooked through, you dip it in a battered egg then in breadcrumbs, and finally you flash fry it to give it its signature flavor. The rice is sweet because of the cinnamon and coconut you put in it. It's an amazing combination of lightly fried crispy chicken and sweet soft rice."

"That sounds incredible," Catalina said flirtatiously. "Have you been able to talk to your family, Marco?"

He let out a sigh and looked down. "I have not spoken to them in so long."

"You must miss them," she said, embracing him. "I'm sure they miss you too."

"Yeah, I know. Do want wine?" Marco said, eager to change the subject. "I have a great bottle of Argentine Malbec I have been saving."

"Absolutely. You have good taste."

"The best," he said with a grin. "I want to show you something, after dinner."

"OK, what?"

"You'll just see after dinner."

"Yes, sir," she said with a smirk.

Time seemed to fly when Marco was with Catalina. He couldn't take his eyes off of her, nor could she take her eyes off him. They flirted incessantly, almost like children on a playground. Before either one knew it, they had polished off the bottle of wine and dinner had concluded.

"You up for a walk?" he asked.

"Are you going to show me that thing?"

"Yes."

"OK, let's go."

He led her down to the beach where the house was to be built. Catalina looked at Marco as if asking why they were standing next to an empty beach. "It's mine," he said, I'm building on it."

"Building what?"

"A house for you and me and our family." Marco put his arms around her.

"Woah, no way. Narco Lord Marco building a home, it sounds too simple," she whispered.

"I need simple sometimes, and I'm not a Narco lord, I'm just Marco. If I could, I would leave the A.U.C. right now."

"Come," she said, sitting on a mound of sand. Marco sat down next to her. "So what's your plan, simple Marco? What would you do if you could leave?"

"There is no way out of the A.U.C unless Costeno lets me out, which I do not see happening. But if I was let out... I don't know. I think about it a lot. I would like to raise a little family here. Coach some soccer. Help my parents. Find a job doing good. Money's no issue now, so I just want to feel good about what I do."

She laid her head on his shoulder. "You have a good heart, Marco. I hope we get that opportunity," she whispered. They sat there in silence for a minute, lit up by the moon and the stars and listening to the waves rumbling onto the shore and the breeze rustling the leaves behind them.

"What do you want?" Marco asked her, breaking the silence.

"I want to be happy."

That's a perfect answer. Marco put his arm around her. She looked up at him. Her face glowed beautifully in the moonlight. He put his other hand on her cheek, leaned in closely, and gently kissed her for the first time in a long time. After a few seconds they pulled apart and he looked into her eyes. "I don't think I could ever get sick of that."

She giggled and smiled at him. "I think you'll get your opportunity, Marco."

"To get sick of kissing you?"

"No!" Catalina said, laughing. "To leave the A.U.C."

"Why do you say that? Have you spoken to your uncle?"

"Yes, you'll be happy to hear he won't be bothering us anymore. His excuse when I confronted him was that he was trying to protect me and that he was looking out for my future. I told him to leave us alone and that I know what's best for my future and myself, for that matter."

"Is that enough to make sure we're both safe?"

"I have that man's heart in the palm of my hand, amor. I've always been like a daughter to him. He won't bother us."

Marco let out a deep breath. It felt like the weight of the world had just been lifted off his shoulders. For the first time in his life, he felt hopeful about his future.

"Tio said the United States is using planes to monitor the coasts and that it's impossible to move shipments. He thinks they know who he is and that they're looking for him. He's constantly on the move with false documents. That's also why we never hear from him. I don't even know where he is right now."

A glimmer of hope began to grow in Marco's chest. "Maybe I will get that opportunity then," he whispered, looking into Catalina's eyes.

"Maybe you will," she whispered back before pushing him down onto the sand, grabbing his neck gently and kissing him slowly and passionately.

CHAPTER TWENTY

ANGELS & DEVILS

As the seasons came and went, the young couple's love truly began to blossom. El Patron was constantly on the run, evading the U.S. government, so his intervention never became a concern, but it was something Marco pondered from time to time. Marco continued building his dream home, and Catalina charged herself with the responsibility of decorating.

It seemed unreal that his life could have been so violent and unpredictable only a couple of months ago and now be so calm and peaceful. For Valentine's Day that year, Marco took Catalina on a beautiful cruise around the Caribbean. And wouldn't you know, nine months later a beautiful baby girl entered the world. She was born on November 12th. They named her Angel. Marco made it a tradition to buy Catalina a rose every month so that she always knew he kept her and their child in his heart, no matter what.

It had been three years since Marco had joined the United Self-Defense Forces of Colombia, but it truly felt like a lifetime. At twenty-four, Marco was no longer a boy but a man with a family to care for, and he was committed to making sure he did just that. Marco had never believed people when they told him everything changes once you're a father, but he had found that to be true. Nothing mattered more to him now than his beautiful baby girl.

Marco finished his home early that winter and moved his family in. He swelled with pride as he cherished the home his hands had built and reflected on the events of the past few years. He was excited to be spending Christmas with his daughter and longed for the chance to introduce her to his parents.

Although content with his current situation, he always knew he was never completely free. The war was still being waged, and he realized that he could be summoned at any time. He knew that, until he lifted that feeling of imprisonment, there would be an unrelenting emptiness inside him.

Marco lay in his bed, with Catalina still asleep at his side, following a nap. The baby was in the other room and it was storming outside as it usually did in the afternoon around this time of year. There was a loud knock on the door, so Marco rolled out of bed and grabbed the trusty pistol he kept on his bedside table. He holstered it behind his back and went to check the front door.

There was another loud knock. "Who is it?" Marco yelled as he walked through the marvelous marble and granite-topped kitchen he had built for himself.

"Oso," replied the visitor on the other side of the door.

Marco hastily opened the door, and two very wet men entered his home: Oso and Carlos Castano. They both removed their raincoats and hung them on the porch next to the door. Marco had not seen or heard from either man in months and neither looked very happy. Their beards had become scruffy, and their hair was uncombed. Their eyes looked tired and baggy, which Marco figured was from the stress and constant movement. Marco was ecstatic to see Oso and was beaming at him.

Carlos looked at Marco and was the first to speak. "Well done, Marco, this is a beautiful house you have built. Is it true that my niece and her daughter are here? They would be a sight for sore eyes."

"Thank you, Patron, and yes, Catalina and our daughter are both here," Marco replied. The Patron flinched as he heard Marco say "our."

"I'll go wake her, please make yourselves comfortable." Marco went into his room. "Amor, you uncle is here," he whispered to Catalina.

Her sleepy eyes rolled up. "Tio? Really?"

"Yes, he would like to see you and the baby."

"OK, I'll be right there, I just need to get dressed," she said excitedly.

Marco went back into the living room, where Oso and El Patron were seated. "It is good to see you gentlemen," Marco said, taking a seat.

"You too, brother," Oso replied with a smile.

Looking around anxiously, as if expecting someone to burst through the door at any moment, Carlos didn't waste a second. "We're here for business and pleasure, Marco. Time is of the essence. I can't stay in one place for too long. I need a captain, a good reliable captain."

Oso interjected, "Our last two shipments have been caught by the Navy." Marco's heart sank as Catalina walked in with the baby.

"TIO!" she exclaimed. "It's so good to see you safe!"

He walked over and gently gave her a hug. "Hola, Hermosa," he crooned to the toddler. "May I hold her?"

"Of course," Catalina said. It was strange for Marco to see Carlos in such a gentle state. He had seen the man murder multiple people, and now he held his child. A primal roar built up in Marco's chest as he watched El Patron rock Angel in his arms.

"What a sight for sore eyes you are," Carlos said to Angel. She started to cry. It gave Marco a bit of satisfaction that his daughter could feel the evil in this man. *She's smart,* he thought proudly.

Catalina gently took over and rocked the baby, whispering a lullaby *"Noni noni a descansar que manana ay que madrugar.* "I'm going to put her to bed. Do you guys want anything? I can make some coffee for you."

"That would be amazing," said Carlos.

"OK." Catalina smiled. "It's so good to see you, Tio." She rushed off to put the baby to bed.

Carlos turned and looked at Marco. He narrowed his eyes and said darkly, "You need not worry about them if something happens to you." Anger swelled inside Marco as he digested those words.

"What are you getting at?"

"Take it for what it's worth. Now, you will leave in two days. That's plenty of time to get your affairs in order."

"And if I refuse?"

"Do not forget why you have this marvelous home, boy," Patron said sharply. "You owe everything to us. You are a member of the A.U.C., and you will do as you are told. I could never harm my own blood, but I can make your life difficult in many other ways."

Marco was sick of this man threatening him. He stood up. "If I do this, I want out." Their whispers were quickly becoming louder.

"You have no right to argue with me, boy. If you want out it'll be in a box. I would kill you for disrespecting me like this if you weren't involved with my niece. Two days. The Finca." Carlos marched toward the front door, pushing past Marco, with Oso trailing behind.

CHAPTER TWENTY-ONE

THE STORM

Marco didn't sleep the next two days. He contemplated his situation throughout the day and lay awake at night carefully weighing all his options. He could refuse and leave the country, but who knew what kind of consequences that would bring. Marco also considered the benefits. Upon completion of the trip, he knew the payout would be enormous. Prices had been skyrocketing for months. He would be able to live the rest of his life very comfortably. Angel would get the best schooling available, and he would be able to give her every opportunity possible.

Reluctantly, and despite Catalina's disapproval, he prepared himself for the journey ahead. It was dusk when Marco had his pack filled with supplies and was in route to the Finca for what Marco hoped would be the last time. He heard thunderstorms rolling in and could feel the air around him cooling. The thunder was loud and massive lightning bolts struck repeatedly in the distant ocean. Droplets of rain began to plop onto the roof of Marco's car. Before long it was coming down in buckets. Marco arrived to the Finca and saw the men packing up the boat. It was the same forty-two-foot-long speedboat he had taken to Honduras, but she had been upgraded to five three-hundred-horsepower engines for this trip. She was definitely built for speed, but a storm like this could produce massive waves, and that was another challenge entirely.

Heavy rain continued to pour down on them as Marco made his way over to the dock where Oso was awaiting him. He was soaked before he had arrived. "What am I bringing?" he asked Oso, putting his hand above his eyes to protect them from the rain.

"Two thousand five hundred kilos," he yelled back. "The storm looks really bad." He looked concerned. "But the best time to move merchandise is when it's rainy and choppy. Much less likely someone will pursue you, and it throws off radar."

Marco laughed. "Only in this situation would someone be happy to see a storm before heading out to sea." He looked at his friend, realizing it may be the last time. "Listen, Oso. I spoke with Catalina, and we would like you to be Angel's Godfather. You have always looked out for me, and I hope if something happens to me you will do the same for her."

Oso looked at Marco affectionately. "It would be my honor, brother." Oso took Marco into a bear hug, squeezing the air out of his lungs. "Be safe out there. Come back safely."

Marco looked out into the ocean and said, "I will, I promise," unsure if he would be able to keep that promise.

Marco rounded up the team of men joining him and boarded the boat. There would be six of them including him. Even tied to the dock the boat swayed angrily back and forth. Marco had never seen a storm like this. Rain was coming down hard from above, and the salty sea threatened to climb aboard from below. The distant sky was draped in complete darkness except for the occasional lightning strike. He thought of his father, who had taught him to sail, and knew he would be furious at him for putting his life in danger like this.

Marco reached into his pocket and pulled out a picture of his little family, taken the day Angel was born, and placed it on the dashboard. "I'll be back. I promise, Angel," he whispered, knowing deep in his bones he would do everything he could to keep his promise. The rain chilled him to the core. "Untie the ropes!" Marco bellowed, watching as his crew sprang into action.

He looked out onto the water and felt the familiar rush returning. Although Marco hated to admit it, the adrenaline was a welcome feeling. It was intoxicating and made him feel more alive than he had felt in a long time. The ropes were untied and Marco sent the boat in reverse. As soon as he was clear of the dock, he put the engines to work, spinning the boat and pulling a 180-degree turn.

The farther from shore he got, the larger the waves became. "HANG ON!" he yelled as the boat climbed up a wave before sliding down the other side. The next surge crashed onto the front of the boat. Water was everywhere on the boat, and the drainage holes could barely keep up with the quantity. Anything that wasn't attached was either floating or had already been thrown off. The storm continued to worsen as Marco forced his vessel onward into the dark merciless sea.

As the hours passed, the only thing that Marco could hear was the waves crashing, one by one, onto the boat. *This is insane,* he thought as a massive wave smashed into them, almost capsizing the boat. *If we encounter one even a little bigger than that we're done. We're dead.* He pushed the boat forward, unsure if he was being brave or stupid. Another wave smashed into the boat, splashing cold salt water everywhere, stinging his eyes and sending shivers down his spine. The wind howled, making communicating with his sailors impossible. He continued forward, becoming less brave by the second, as wave after wave crashed into the boat. Just when Marco thought things couldn't get any worse, lightning struck twenty yards to the left of them, lighting up the sky. Briefly he could see the terrified faces of his men as they clung on for dear life to whatever they could.

He looked at the picture of Angel in front of him. "No, I will not die today." He started turning the boat around. The men cheered, grateful to be heading out of this suicide mission. He had to be careful and time the turn precisely to avoid being upturned, which would all but guarantee death by drowning. No man could survive in this water. Marco waited patiently until he found the perfect wave and steered the boat back toward shore just before the wave came crashing down. The ride back was not a smooth one. Rain made visibility almost non-existent, and the force of each wave relentlessly rocked the boat back and forth. Marco gripped the wheel as hard as he could to keep the boat straight and prayed that they would not be struck by lightning.

Marco headed toward the faint lights of the Finca, maneuvering his ship through the colossal storm. With each passing moment the light became slightly larger. It gave him hope and he continued to move forward. The engines roared, forcing water out of their path. As they got closer to shore, it was almost as if they were surfing the waves back to the coastline. The light continued to grow, welcoming them home.

He thought of his family once again and pushed the boat forward, sounding the horn. Hearing them return, ship hands on shore ran out to the dock to throw them rope. His sailors immediately tied them down and ran for shore. They kissed the dock, when they arrived on solid land, and ran home to their wives and children, grateful to be alive. Marco was the last to disembark and, as he walked up the beach, he walked into a swaying Patron.

Carlos had a bottle of tequila in his left hand and a pistol in his right hand. "WHY ARE YOU HERE!" He pointed the pistol at Marco.

"We were going to die out there," he pleaded over the wind, trying to reason with the drunken drug lord.

"THEN YOU SHOULD HAVE DIED. KILL OR BE KILLED. THAT'S NARCO LAW!" El Patron moved closer to him, pistol still raised.

"I HAVE A FAMILY, I WILL NOT DROWN IN THE OCEAN!" Marco yelled back.

El Patron moved in closer and jammed the pistol into Marco's ribs. He was only inches from his face, and Marco could smell the tequila on his breath "YOU WILL DIE TODAY!"

Marco glared back at one of the most feared men in Colombia, looking him straight in the eyes. He had had enough. He had reached his breaking point; he would no longer let this man control his life. "FINE, KILL ME THEN, I'VE BEEN DEAD A LONG TIME. I WOULD RATHER BE DEAD. THIS ISN'T LIVING. I'M TIRED OF THE ABUSE AND CONSTANTLY WORRYING ABOUT WHETHER I'M

GOING TO BE KILLED OR NOT. ITS BETTER IF YOU KILL ME, I'M READY TO DIE!"

El Patron drew back his pistol in surprise. He let out a sigh. "Get some rest, Niño, you can leave when the storm settles." El Patron turned around and stumbled away. Marco took a deep breath and made his way to his car. He got in and was about to turn on the ignition when a young man tapped on the window.

"Marco!"

"What?" Marco lowered the window. It was Nico.

"You look tired, man," Nico said coolly.

"I haven't slept in two days." Marco was shocked to see Nico. "How are you, Nico?"

"I have been better, brother." Nico was soaked and had bags in his eyes.

"What's up, man?"

Nico looked him in the eyes. "I lost my last shipment, Marco, and need to pay back The Patron or I'm going to end up like Pitufo. I would like to transport that for you. I need the money, please. We'll split it fifty-fifty, please."

CHAPTER TWENTY-TWO

SOARING

The next evening the storm had settled. Nico boarded the speedboat and headed to Mexico with the crew while Marco sat comfortably on his patio drinking a glass of red wine. He had never been so happy to be home as he had been the previous night. He had spent hours just watching Angel sleep, grateful for the opportunity to be her father. Catalina couldn't have been happier to have him home and hadn't left his side all night.

El Patron had cleared Nico taking the merchandise that morning. He didn't care who took the cocaine to Mexico as long as it got there, but he made it clear it would be Marco's responsibility if it didn't.

A few mornings passed and Marco was awoken by the telephone ringing. "Hola?"

"Buenos Dias, Marco, it's Oso. I have regrettable news. Nico had engine troubles on his way back in Belize. We're sending you to take care of it."

"Son of a bitch," Marco said, rubbing his eyes.

"We're sending a car, so be ready."

"OK, adios," Marco grumbled. He hung up the phone and stared out the sliding glass door that overlooked the ocean.

"What happened?" a sleepy Catalina asked.

"Nico's engines went down, I'm flying to Belize tonight."

"*Hijo de puta*," she swore. She crawled up next to him and laid her head on his chest.

"Be careful, we need you here," she whispered. She never told him not to go. He appreciated that she knew he had to and never made him feel guilty.

"Te amo." He held her tight.

She looked up at him with her beautiful eyes and, in her sweet voice, said, "You know, baby, there are many kinds of love."

"Oh yeah? What kinds?"

She smiled and said softly, "There's love for one's friends, brothers, sisters, mother, fathers, and friends, which can end. But then there's divine love. Which is God's love, it's endless and unrelenting. That's how I love you, forever, always, and no matter what." She kissed him passionately on the lips.

A red Volkswagen car pulled up to the house about an hour later, which had given Marco time to shower and ready himself for the voyage. He had packed his essentials, and he got into the backseat of the car. "Where are we headed?" he asked the driver.

"The airstrip."

Marco nodded and leaned back. He noticed two suitcases lying on the seat. He opened one, revealing rows of hundred-dollar bills. "How much is this?" Marco asked the driver.

"El Patron said half a million in each, Jefe, in case you need it to get back." *El Patron really wants this cargo.* Marco stared out the window, ready for this trip to be over.

They arrived at a clearing a short time later and saw a single-engine plane awaiting them. A white man in yellow sweater and wearing aviator sunglasses awaited them. "That's your ride, Jefe." The driver pointed to the plane. Marco had never been on a plane before and was becoming increasingly anxious. He always thought his first time on a plane would be going to some extraordinary place like Miami or London on a large, safe jet, not Belize on a two-seater airplane that looked like it would fall right out of the sky.

The driver pulled up next to the plane and wished Marco a safe flight.

"Gracias, amigo," he responded, trying not to sound nervous.

The pilot greeted Marco with a smile and a firm handshake. "How are you? My name is George. I will be your pilot today." He was obviously American. "Ready to roll?" The pilot's poise eased Marco's worries, and he began to get excited.

"Let's do it," Marco replied with a smile. George helped Marco put the suitcases into the plane and then jumped on board. Marco put his seatbelt on and tried to relax.

"Here, take this." George handed Marco a headset. Marco put them on, happy to find they blocked sound and helped him hear George more clearly. "Check, check," the pilot said while he fiddled with the gears and knobs.

"Well, being that there's no radio tower we need to wait on, we can go whenever we want, this place is awesome.

It's like there's no rules," he said, laughing. He turned on the plane and let the engine warm up for a minute before beginning to gain speed. Marco clutched the armrests and tried to control his breathing.

"HERE WE GO!" George shouted as the plane's wheels began to lift off from the ground. Marco was yelling and felt a strange sensation in his stomach as the plane began to take off. It was exhilarating. "WOOOO!" they shouted as they climbed higher and higher toward the clouds.

"I need to get one of these!" Marco shouted to George through the headset. Marco was all smiles.

George laughed. "I highly recommend it. You're free when you can fly, no one can hold you down." Those words hit home for Marco. He wanted to be free and, soon, he hoped he would be.

CHAPTER TWENTY-THREE

BELIZE

Marco arrived in Belize late that night after a bumpy but relatively quick flight. He had gotten some sleep on the trip, after the initial excitement of flying had worn off, so he was alert and ready to go, especially after experiencing landing for the first time. Nico had arranged pick up and was waiting for him at the airport. Marco had learned to prefer working under cover of night, as there were always fewer people around. "What's wrong with the engines?" Marco asked as they headed to the docks.

"They're fried," Nico said. "I was moving full throttle the whole time I was in the gulf, no way I was letting those gringos catch me." Marco could hear the anxiety in his voice.

"I don't blame you," Marco said. "You would probably get thirty years in the United States for what you were moving."

"You have no idea, wait until you see the stuff we're bringing back this time. They didn't only pay in cash, Marco."

"What did they give you?"

Nico's face was unusually serious as he turned to face Marco. "A dozen rocket launchers, crates full of grenades, and three hundred assault rifles, plus cash."

"Jesus..." was all Marco could muster.

"The grenade launchers are gorgeous," Nico said with a grin. "We can do some serious damage with those."

They arrived at the docks where the boat was being held. It was tied up and swaying gently as the waves rocked it. The sailors waited patiently for news or instructions on what to do next.

Marco quickly inspected the engines, confirming what Nico had told him. "You're lucky you made it in to a dock and didn't get stuck out there. We need to count inventory. We might as well do that until daybreak. No one is going to the sell us a boat in the middle of the night."

The men got to work counting the inventory. *It's amazing what people would trade for some white powder,* thought Marco as he looked over the armory of weapons he would now need to transport back to Colombia.

Hours passed as they counted and recounted. Finally, day broke and Marco said, "Let's get a new boat and go home." The two Narcos hopped off the boat and went into town to find a local boat shop. They found a rundown building with a large sign up front that read "The Sailors." The lot in the back had half a dozen boats: five smaller fishing boats and one larger one Marco thought may be just big enough to utilize.

The two Colombians walked into the shop. It was a classic fishing shop with everything you might need, from live to bait to snorkeling gear. Marco walked up to the counter and rang the service bell. A tall dark man appeared, chewing a toothpick, wearing a large T-shirt and sporting dreadlocks. "Hello der, how may I be of service to you?" he said with a Caribbean accent. *He's probably from Jamaica.*

"Good morning, we would like to inspect that large fishing boat you have in your lot." "The forty-eight-footer, eh, she's a beaut. A bit pricy though, you sure you have the capital?"

"That's not a problem, show me the boat please," Marco replied with a chuckle, eager to get this over with and head home.

"Very well, follow me." The Jamaican man brought them out to the boat yard where Marco began inspecting the boat's frame. It was a massive white fishing boat with a spacious interior that could fit six comfortably overnight. Perfect for moving merchandise. A ladder led to a second floor, to help the captain navigate. Marco continued inspecting the boat and moved to examine the engines while the Jamaican spoke. "She is in fine condition, worked on her myself. She'll help you catch anything you need or get wherever you need to go with whatever you need to take."

Marco was impressed. She seemed perfect. "How much?"

"Seven hundred thousand dollars."

"I'll give you seven hundred fifty thousand dollars in cash, but I need you to put in two more three-hundred-horsepower engines and have it in the water by tonight."

The islander scratched his chin as he thought. "OK, it can be done. Bring the cash tonight. We will meet you at Dock 7C." The men shook hands and the Jamaican got to work.

CHAPTER TWENTY-FOUR

THE BATTLE

Come nightfall the Narcos loaded the new vessel with their lethal cargo as quickly as they could in order to be on the water by midnight. The cargo was loaded, one by one, as the minutes ticked by. They had clear seas and were able to leave Belize just before midnight. Marco was standing on the bow with the salty wind blowing in his face, flapping back his hair. He shouted to Nico, "We should be at the Finca by daybreak."

"No, Marco. This shipment is going to San Pablo."

"San Pablo? That's where I'm from!" The idea of being in his hometown, even if it was only for a short time, made Marco smile. It had been years since he had been home. His heart swelled with excitement.

The overnight trip went smoothly as they quickly cruised through the water, approaching Marco's home. He debated whether he would sneak away for a few hours and visit his parents before heading back to the Finca. *What will my parents say? How will I explain to them where I have been and why I have not contacted them? My mom will be so disappointed... but I have to tell them about my new family.* He imagined his father holding his baby girl and his mother meeting Catalina. Marco was overcome with emotion as he envisioned all the possible scenarios for his return home.

The sun was beginning to rise as if welcoming them home. They began sailing into the cove of San Pablo. It was beautiful and untouched by mankind with blue water with such clear visibility you could see the ocean floor. Mountains surrounded them just past the sandy beaches. They slowed the boat down to glide through the cove, preventing them from creating too much wake. *We did it!* Marco kicked his feet up and sat back in his chair. He let out a deep breath and his body relaxed. He had made it back safe and sound. He would earn his prize.

Just when Marco thought they were completely out of danger, he began to hear motors. He turned his head and peered into the distance, toward the noise. He saw one speedboat behind them, about a kilometer away, coming in from the left, and a second at an equal distance closing in from the right. On either side of him he heard the roaring of more engines. Trucks outfitted with high-caliber machine guns pulled up on the sides of the beach and drove alongside the boat, maintaining their speed. Marco could see these men were wearing camos, and their sudden appearance had sent his mind racing. *Who are they?* He leaned closer and squinted, trying to get a closer look. Perhaps El Patron had sent a team to meet them. Marco was greeted with gunfire. Marco didn't need to see any more. He knew exactly who they were: the FARC.

"GET THE GUNS!" Marco shouted to the men as they ran inside to arm themselves. Bullets began to fly as gunmen shot at them from all sides, hammering the hull of the boat. There were men on both banks with assault rifles, and the boats behind them began to open fire. They were trapped in a hornet's nest as bullets buzzed by, destroying everything in their path.

Marco jumped down into the cabin and grabbed an AK-47. He loaded it, stuck it outside, and blindly began shooting toward the banks, screaming every curse he could at his attackers. "DIE MOTHERFUCKERSSSS!" He quickly ran out of bullets and dashed inside to grab another clip to return fire. Men were screaming as metal penetrated flesh on both sides. Blood began to spill on the boat deck, making everything slippery.

Marco's men threw grenades at the men on the land. Marco watched as explosions sent metal and fire in all directions. There were dozens of them on each bank. Marco and his men took cover behind the hull of the boat. Marco was about to reach for another mag when he remembered the rocket launchers.

He moved the crates covering the encased rockets and ripped off the cover that read "Bonitas." He grabbed the weapon and put it over his shoulder. The Bonita's immense weight surprised him. He ran to the back of the boat and aimed at one of the approaching boats. Sweat dripped down his forehead, and his heart was beating so fast he felt it would explode. He took a deep breath and pulled the trigger. The force of the propulsion sent him back a step, and the rocket collided into the boat, engulfing it in a ball of flame and sending pieces of men and boat into a watery grave.

"AHHHH!" Marco screamed in pain as a bullet caught him in the back of his left shoulder. He dove forward for cover and clutched his wound. Blood was spilling and it burned. He did not know how they could survive this. The other men continued to launch rockets at the attackers on land. There were explosions everywhere, destroying everything in sight. Their attackers were like ants; they were everywhere, firing unending rounds at Marco and his men. Marco's heart sank as he heard more engines approaching, Marco feared the worst: the FARC had called for more reinforcements. He turned over to see what was happening and saw one of his men, lifeless, hanging over the edge of the railing. More corpses floated on the water, and even more were on land. Injured men screamed and crawled toward amputated body parts, desperate for medical attention. Marco could see they were easily outnumbered twenty-five to one.

Suddenly the guerillas stopped firing upon the boat. Marco took the opportunity to reload the rocket launcher, aim, and fire upon the second encroaching boat. BOOM! Bull's eye. The boat was sent into a fiery inferno. It had never stood a chance against the Bonita.

The guerillas had turned their backs toward the water and were shooting into the jungle. Shouting men and vehicles emerged from the forest, firing onto their attackers. From a distance he saw familiar faces. Daniel was firing like a madman, with an M16, at the trucks on the back of an ATV. Oso was on the back of an armored Jeep firing a fifty-caliber machine gun, mowing down anything that crossed his path.

It wasn't FARC reinforcements; it was his cartel. Scores of A.U.C. spilled out of the jungle, taking the guerillas from behind and tearing them to shreds with bullets. Nico continued firing rockets, alongside Marco, onto their enemies on the beach. The sand was drenched with blood, as dozens of men lay lifeless on the beach, turning the sand pink. The battle continued.

Marco and Nico let out a cheer as their side began to win the battle. Many of the FARC tried to run toward the water and were cut down. The battle had soon been won as the enemy was pinched between the ocean and a wall of bullets. All the men cheered and fired their weapons into the air. "YESSSS!" Marco and Nico screamed. They flung their arms in the air, cheering, ecstatic to be alive. A shot of pain reminded Marco of his wound. He went back over to the controls and maneuvered the boat to the dock. All the men who had just saved his life were waiting.

They were all cheering and hugging. Some continued to shoot their guns into the air and dance, drunk off the victory of battle. Oso and Daniel ran over to Nico and Marco and embraced them. "How did they know we would be here?! How did you know they knew?!" Marco asked.

"It's Colombia," Oso said with a chuckle. "You just need to know who to talk to."

The men began to unload the boat and examine the new toys the A.U.C. had just received from the Mexicans. Older men and young boys upgraded from pistols to AK-47s. "We need to get you looked at, Marco." Oso tore off a piece of his shirt to wrap around the wound on his shoulder, to stop the bleeding.

Marco looked up and saw The Patron overlooking his men, dressed in all camo just like his men. Their eyes met and he motioned for Marco to come to him. "I'll be right back," Marco said to his friends. He climbed up the sandy beach and stood next to Carlos Castano. They overlooked the scenes of men and boys celebrating as others lay dying. Some of their lives merely beginning while others had been ruthlessly ended.

"What is it you want now?" Marco asked Carlos.

"Relax, Marco, if I wanted you dead you would already be dead." *He's right.*

"Fuck those guys," Marco said to Castano.

"They are not so different from you and I, Marco. They drink the same water and eat the same food. They feel happiness, fear, sadness, warmth, and cold just as you or I. They do what they do for a better life, for themselves or for their children. We must forgive because when you forgive, you love, and when you love, God's light shines on you."

Marco was taken aback. He had never heard anything like that come from The Patron; he was a man of many layers. "What is it you want, Marco?"

"Nothing, Patron." Knowing full well what he wanted only came with him in a box.

"Come on, Marco, what do you want?"

"Just my pay, Jefe."

Carlos Castano looked him up and down. "You are my nephew now, be a man and ask me for what you want."

Marco, exhausted from battle, used his last ounce of energy to muster up all the courage within him. He looked The Patron in the eye and said, "I want out, I want my freedom."

Castano glared back at him and clenched his jaw. The two men stared into each other's souls. Carlos broke eye contact, looked out into the sea, and smiled. "Granted," he said turning back to Marco. "Now get out of here, go collect your things and say goodbye. Go take care of my niece and your baby."

Marco's eyes widened; he couldn't believe it. He looked at Carlos and said, "Thank you, Tio." The men shook hands, for the first time, as equals before Carlos took his leave. Marco turned and looked down at the men who had come to his rescue as they celebrated down by the beach. He watched the waves crash into the sand and the sunlight glimmer on the water in the distance. He smelled the salt in the air and watched as the breeze rustled the treetops that grew on the mountains. It was as if he were experiencing the world for the first time. He felt the weight he had carried on his shoulders since that first night in The Patron's garage lift off of him. Tears filled his eyes and gratitude filled his heart. Today was the best day of his life. He was a free man. He was going home.

FIN

Acknowledgements

First and foremost to every single one of you for choosing to read this book, thank you so much. It means the world to me. I hope you enjoy it.

To my mom & dad for the unconditional love you have so selflessly given Blake and me since the moment you became our mommy and daddy and for every nugget of golden wisdom you have shared with us. Any success we obtain is a direct reflection of your love and commitment to our family. I love you forever, always, and no matter what. Thank you from the bottom of my heart.

Blakey Cakey – Thank you for always being there for me and for being the best friend and brother a guy could ask for. I am very proud of you and am very excited for what the future has in store for us. When I win, you win. Your contributions to this book are invaluable, and I couldn't have done it without your constant support and suggestions. I love you forever, always, and no matter what.

My Whole Family - Thank you for all the love, laughs, glasses of wine, hospitality, honesty, and support. I couldn't have done it without you.

Marco - Thank you for entrusting me with the incredible story of your life. Few men could live in multiple lifetimes the amount you fit into one; you are a constant source of inspiration to me.

To my students - Don't just follow your dreams; chase them relentlessly and demand that the universe make them a reality. You deserve it.

Special thanks to:

Nick Page & Daniel Garcia for being the friends every young man deserves to have and for having my back throughout our Colombian adventures. And an extra special thanks to you guys for examining and improving every single word of this novel with me in order to make it the best it could be; I genuinely could not have done it without you. A la orden, siempre. To Hannah Wilhjelm, thank you for inspiring so effortlessly and for your contributions to this novel. You are incredible. My hope for you is that you learn to let your own light shine and find in yourself the divinity I saw in you the first time our eyes locked. To Alex Marciniak, you are a saint and the nicest person I know. Thank you for always being there for me during the good and the bad times. To Paige Kauffman for her selflessness and priceless contributions. And to Brian Aldrich, thank you for reminding me to always remain true to myself and for being an overall gangster.

To all my friends - Knowing that I have so many people in my life to be thankful for humbles me and makes my heart overflow with gratitude. Each one of you has made a priceless impact on me that I will forever cherish. I'll do my best not to forget anyone. The C-Boyz, that's fam, thanks for being the best friends a guy could ask for and for being there for my family and me when we needed you most. The

Marcus Family, Top Tier, Pi Kappa Alpha, Heart for Change fellows, especially Mike Love and Cam Evans. Tampa Bay Buccaneers interns, Saint Pete fam, Olympic Heights Varsity Football and Lacrosse, SGA, my Halo friends, and an extra special thanks to my friends from middle school who loved me even though I was a nerd which, by the way, is the coolest thing you can be.

To my Coaches and Teachers- Susan Klevansky, you are a saint and it was a pleasure to be your student. Daniel Cowan for going above and beyond for me since the first day of class. Coaches and mentors: Nate Feilich, Alex Grokhowsky, Mitch Henghold, Steven Sigmund, Casey Palacious, Jack Siney, and Paul Farese. Sir Vince Cohen. Mickey Farrell, Maureen Myers, Kevin Brown, Christy Schnell, Steve Fidura, Mark Dominic and Brian Ford.

All of you have made a tremendous impact on my life and I could not have done this without your lessons, support, discipline, and encouragement. Thank you to everyone, once again. Love you all.